CINDERFELLA

Xavier Neal
International Best Selling Author

Cinderfella
By Xavier Neal
©Xavier Neal 2015
All Rights Reserved
Cover by Entertwine Publishing

ISBN-13:
978-1514178843
ISBN-10:
1514178842

License Note
No part of this book may be reproduced, scanned, or distributed in any printed or electronic form with authorization of the Author Xavier Neal.

This book is a work of fiction. Names, characters, places, and incidents are either the product of the author's imagination or are used fictitiously, and any resemblance to actual persons, living or dead, events, or locales is entirely coincidental.

Chapter 1

Apparently I managed to piss off the winds of change while I was sleeping last night because instead of the opportunity of a lifetime to really win this scholarship, I want, no, fuck that, I need, I'm now more likely to win a certificate for best dressed senior in my holey jeans and stained white t-shirts.

"To hell I will!" Gianna, aka the reason my shot at something more than community college is now in shambles, like One Direction fans after that one dude left, throws her French manicured hands up in protest. She's sitting in the back row. Corner. The one seat in the entire theater classroom we've deemed the throne of the pointless. It's where seniors sit who just need a credit to pass. The rest of us are devoted to this. Determined that we were meant to take this path. Truth? Acting may be my biggest dream and what I figured I would get a scholarship for, but I plan to minor in something that's more stable. I need something more stable. Doesn't mean I can't keep hope to have my career take off.

"Do not talk like that in my classroom," Ms. Flores, the lead theater director snaps back, putting a hand on her hip. "You'll be partners with Connor."

Can someone else be Connor?

"What did I just say?" Gianna snidely responds.

Ms. Flores points sternly. "My office. Now."

"I hate this school," she growls, tosses her hot pink purse, and stands. Our eyes having no choice but to watch her tantrum like it's a car wreck on the major highway and we have nowhere else to look. The sound of her heels clicking across the tile are equivalent to nails on a chalkboard at this point.

Yup. My teacher picks the bitchiest girl with the least amount of potential in the whole class to be my partner. She is constantly saying how much confidence and faith she has in me. Yet when the perfect opportunity comes along for her to prove that by pairing me with Stacey McDougal, who's predicted to be the next Natalie Portman, what does she do? She sticks me with a video ho' whose extent of acting probably doesn't stretch further than the bedroom. Yup. Fuck the winds of change. I should've never counted on them blowing a direction that would help someone like me.

"Now that that's settled," she returns talking to us. "I'd like to just remind you all how important it is to try your very best. Every year schools from all around the state go to compete for the chance at this scholarship. Now everyone here in Stage Acting has the talent and skills to win and by traditional standards, I expect we'll bring home a trophy of some sort, and one of you that scholarship."

I had the same belief until about three minutes ago.

"I hate this school!" Gianna yells from the office.

Until that loud mouthed purse accessory was picked to be my partner. Uncomfortable, I slide down further into my chair.

"You have four months. The competition is the first weekend in May. You'll be required to perform in the competition. This will stand in place of your final. If for some reason there is an emergency, and you cannot make it, you will be judged on your rehearsal performance that takes place in front of your peers the night before. So, with that announced, I encourage all of you to try your absolute hardest, pick the finest duet scenes you can, and pour all of your effort into them, because if you let it, this project can really change your lives."

For the worse. This project will change some of our lives for the worse is what she should've said. Particularly my life. Score.

"On that note, I want you to break up into your teams and start searching for your pieces."

Everyone scatters allowing me to take my opportunity to have a word with my beautiful Hispanic teacher, who I still have a heavy crush on even after two years.

"Ms. Flores," my voice hums. "About this partner situation…"

Twisting her dark brown, blonde highlighted hair, into a bun she sighs, "You're wondering if there was a reason I paired you up the way I did, aren't you?"

"Yeah. I mean usually you have a motive--"

"I always have a motive."

"Right. But this—"

"Trust me," she cuts me off. My eyes take the breathing moment to wander over her body that's in great shape despite her age. Her small yet perky boobs have my attention thanks to her scoop neck shirt I'm sure doesn't fit into the school dress code. Not that I'm complaining. Hell, I don't know anyone who would.

"I do. Really. This just doesn't feel right."

"Well maybe a little wrong is something it's time for you to try," she gives me a little wink. "Now if you'll excuse me, I need to go have a word with your just as excited partner."

Trust her? She says trust her? She put me with a girl whose only in this class because when they transferred her from the last place I'm sure the royal bitch deemed unworthy, it was the only elective open in her block of time. I don't even know if she can act since the semester started with a research paper. And try a little wrong? Is she joking? There's so much wrong in my life that anymore and Shakespeare would classify me as a tragedy.

Folding my hands in a frustrated fashion on top of my head, I lean up against the side of the wall right outside of her office. I make sure to stay where I can't be seen. It's a perfect eavesdropping location. Not sure I wanna hear what is about to be said though.

"Do we have a problem?" Ms. Flores says, her tone firm and strict.

"Obviously we do."

"Which is?"

"You wanna pair me with the diamond in the rough instead of a prize winning piece."

"Sometimes the most beautiful diamonds are the ones that were roughest first."

"No." Gianna snips. "Don't give me some after school special crap please. I'm being real with you, give me the same courtesy. You want me paired with 2 dollar wine when I deserve 200 dollar champagne. I'm steak. That's chicken fried steak."

Not sure which part of that pisses me off most, I drop my hands and turn to lean my shoulder against the wall. No, I don't get to dress like the Ken dolls she's probably used to being seen with, but that doesn't mean I'm not attractive. And if that's the case, then why do I always have a list of girlfriends anxious for me to ask them out come every Friday?

Annoyed Ms. Flores sighs, "Connor, by traditional standards is amazing. He's talented, genuine, and charming. By this societies standards he's exceptional—"

"Exceptionally lame."

"Exceptionally bright and is predicted to be an Oscar winner very early in his career. He's one of the best performers we have and you should feel humbled by being with such a presence."

"Oh please. Humbled?"

"By what his clothing" There's a short pause. "And he's not the only one with skills."

"You're right Gianna. I've seen your written records and some of the recordings. You have some talent too. If you two pick the right scene the amount of griping and complaining you do might just come in handy." Her sarcasm makes me smirk.

"I don't want to be partners with him." God. You would think the way she's talking about me, I have the plague or something.

"Alright."

"Alright."

"I respect your choice."

"Good."

"You can go see Mr. Smith in his office once more and see if he'll let you stay here in his school, which if I'm correct is the last chance before you're shipped away to boarding school in Canada? Or was it Wales?"

"Wait. Wait. Wait…" Gianna's voice suddenly lacks in defense. "Let's not get so hasty…"

"Oh now that's hasty? I was under the impression the way you were speaking about Connor, a student you know nothing about, was hasty." Before Gianna has a chance to fire back, she states, "Now, you're going to go in there, force a fake smile on your face, and be his partner. You're going to give this an actual shot or I will not hesitate to call Mr. Smith to start the paperwork to have you removed from not only my class, but the school. Are we clear?"

Her gum pops before she sighs, "Crystal."

"Good," Ms. Flores' voice perks up, which is when I move away quickly to my seat where I pretend to be zipping up my navy blue backpack.

Without so much as a glance, Gianna strolls back up to her chair where she plops down, grabs her purse, and begins rummaging around in it.

Nodding to myself that this is going to be successful, I grab my backpack, walk up the side stairs to the top of the seating area, and sit beside her. At first she stares at me blankly like I'm joking around by being in her presence, which is quickly replaced by disgust.

"Can I help you?" she sneers, smacking her gum at me before crossing her bare coffee colored legs that are barely being covered by a pink and black pleated school girl skirt, which I admit has my attention.

"My name's Connor," I extend my hand for her to shake exposing my own tan skin that's golden from hours of outside labor.

Her dark brown eyes glare at my hand before looking back up at me. "Connor? Isn't that something you name your kid when you and your lover can't come to an agreement?"

My lips press together before I smile sarcastically. "Gianna right?" She gives me a slight nod and I sigh, "Isn't that what you name your child when you want her to grow up to be a stripper?"

"Is there a reason you're bothering me?"

"We're supposed to be partners," my annoyance for her grows faster and faster with every bat of her long brown eyelashes. "Remember what Ms. Flores said in her office?"

Clearly irritated she adjusts the top half of her wardrobe now, "You were eavesdropping."

"I prefer to call it overhearing."

"Call it what you like, but you were sticking your nose where it didn't belong. Haven't you ever heard of privacy?"

"She left her door open. I count that as public."

"Well then you heard me tell her I won't work with someone like you."

"And what makes me so unacceptable to you?"

"The fact you mix your Wal-Mart and K-mart brand clothes is a start."

Biting my tongue I reply, "Well not all of us can only worry about which designer impostor perfume is going to match the day's slutty outfit. Some of us have real world shit to deal with."

"Contemplating if it's really beef or just a substitute hardly qualifies as real world shit to deal with." She pops a bubble in my face right as the bell rings.

"Well this has been as much fun as being kicked in the nuts, so if you'll excuse me." I slip my backpack over one shoulder. "I have somewhere to be."

"Is the thrift store having a buy one get one sale?" she giggles at her comment. Rolling my eyes, I slide down the railing. On my way out of the room, I swallow the lump of hatred that's managed to form in such a small amount of time. No reason to be surprised by her behavior. Most girls who look that hot act that bitchy. They can afford to. On all levels. I do my best to push any more thoughts of her out of my mind as I hustle to the student parking lot, praying I can show up to work early for once.

Hopping into my hunter green 2007 Volkswagen Jetta, I start the car and take off out of the parking lot waving goodbye to Mr. Johnson, the parking lot attendant. At the first stop light I rip off my plain white colored t-shirt I wore to school and slide on my navy blue polo. When I reach the next light, I apply deodorant and refresh my breath with the last of the tic-tacs I ate for lunch today. Even though I did the best I could to change in the car instead of stopping to do it in the bathroom, I still arrive at work one minute late.

After typing the code into the private preschool, I stroll right up to the time clock machine. "Good afternoon Nelly."

Nelly is often the saving grace of this place. She keeps the parents happy and the teachers happier. The friendly face where all problems seem to go to die. The blonde hair, the pale skin, and her constant preference to wear white uniform shirts gives off the allure of an angel.

"Good afternoon." She smiles, leaning over the office desk, her pregnant belly basically sitting on top of it. "How are you?"

"Good. And you?"

"Better now that you're here." Her simple wink lets me know I've got my work cut out for me today. Because of the math test I'm pretty sure I failed and the devil who has the most gorgeous pair of legs I've ever seen weren't enough trouble for one day. Damn. I thought that girl was out of my mind. Shaking away the thought of her, I watch Nelly slide a piece of paper over to me. "By the way your collar is tucked in your shirt."

"Damn," I mumble and quickly fix my collar.

"Get dressed in a hurry?"

"Always." I softly smirk. Reviewing the list of repairs I grumble, "God, what's the deal? Did everything in the school break this morning?"

"Looks that way doesn't it?" Nelly leans back in her chair to answer the phone. "Sunshine and Rainbows, this is Nelly speaking, how may I help you?" After a beat she says, "Yes, I sure can. Just give me one moment please." Hitting the hold button, she says to me, "Mr. Harrison would like to talk to you in his office."

"Great…" my mumble is chuckled at. Any time Mr. Harrison, the owner, wants to talk it usually ends with 'Do I need to hire someone else?' It's like he thinks the only way he can talk to me is by threatening my job at the end. Luckily for me, Mrs. Evans, the school director, loves me and does her best to always save me. One of the few people in my life, next to Nelly, who always tries to help.

Slowly, I walk into the office, which is the size of a shoe box if you ask me, directly behind Nelly and close the clear door. Nelly smiles and gives me a slight wave as I divert my attention to the owner and director who I feel are scolding me every other week for something.

"I'm glad you're here on time today," Mr. Harrison, who reminds me of a slightly less awesome version of Clint Eastwood, leans back in his black leather office chair, that owning one of the most prestigious preschools in the state helped him buy. That chair alone could probably cover the grocery bill in my house for weeks.

"I try sir. Sometimes it's hard when I get out of class late or there's bad traffic, but I try sir. I really do. And if this is about that then—"

"It's not." Mrs. Evans, our very own Mary Poppins, as the teachers call her behind her back, shakes her head leaning back in her matching leather chair clicking off her computer. "In fact this is actually a good meeting."

"Really?" my confusion amuses both of them.

"Yes." Mr. Harrison nods folding his hands into his lap. "I know sometimes it feels like all I do is gripe at you, but I just strive for you to be better. To be better. This is an amazing school, and you've contributed quite a lot to it I realize, but I only want the best of the best at all times. You don't win that many awards and acclamations conducting yourself at half of your potential. With that said, corporate was in earlier today and mentioned how clean and well running the school was, despite the few bumps on your to do list of course. I know you don't strictly clean, since I have a cleaning crew, and I know you don't repair everything since there's parts you have to be certified for, but you keep the school working and clean on a daily basis until the professionals get here, which speaks highly of you and us. It pleased corporate, which means it pleased me."

"Well thank you," I politely reply.

"We'll be giving you a dollar raise and a larger discount here at the school," Mrs. Evans exclaims cheerfully. "And I know that'll be a great help to you."

Standing up I nod. "Thank you both very much. This...this means a lot to me."

"Get started on that list." Mr. Harrison winks at me and turns back around to his computer.

I exit the office with the sheet of paper still in my hand and stroll by Nelly who's smiling widely.

"See, it's not always a bad trip to the office when you go," she giggles pressing her lips to her water bottle.

"The Principal's office is the Principal's office no matter which way you say it." When she laughs again, I smile widely. "Better get started on these repairs. How did the toddlers break the bookshelf again?"

"They're toddlers Connor. That's what they do."

"Yeah, yeah, yeah, don't I know it," I mutter heading down the hallway.

As I start down the long hallway passing brightly painted walls, where beautiful crafted kid art is hanging and bulletin boards containing monthly themes to present to the parents, I smirk widely to myself. The first break I've had in a long time. It feels good. Hell, it feels fantastic. Maybe God is trying to balance out the hell he stuck me in earlier with Gianna by helping out the rest of my life. Then again if he were really trying to help he could've given me a break by letting me have a real partner or at least let that girl wear an outfit that covers more of those long coffee legs. They're fucking perfect. Why give her perfect legs and an imperfect mouth? Ha. That's balance.

Passing by the younger classrooms I wave at teachers who see me stroll by their windows. At the end of the hall, I take a left heading towards the older kid's playground. With a small smile I prepare myself for what's going to be a long afternoon of fixing everything from creaky swings to leaky kitchen faucets.

While I'm outside on the older children's playground fixing the loose tire swing, they come running outside to play a little earlier than they are scheduled to. I place a smile on my face, greeting the kids as they greet me with hellos and hugs. Within a matter of moments their teacher sees me, politely saying hello too.

"You look hard at work," Kendall McGee saunters over to me, her twenty five year old hips allowing her black dress pants to dangle off them to reveal a slight midriff, which if I didn't know any better, I swear I could see the hint of a dangling belly button ring. Can't deny the woman is attractive, but much like my theater teacher that's a crush that should stay that way.

"Trying," I sigh, the Texas late winter sun being hot enough to make me sweat yet not enough to warm up the place. "It seems like everything broke down while I was away today."

"Just about," she giggles, tossing her strawberry blonde feathered hair out of her face. "Something else around here could use a little a fixing…"

A small smile creeps across my face. "Oh yeah? What's that?"

With her hands tugging at her white sweater sleeves, she slides next to me, allowing me to hover over her at 6'2. After glancing at the children who seem to be enjoying the fresh air, she less than innocently leans in. "Me."

My screwdriver almost slides out of my hand, "Really?"

"And I think the sooner the better," she sweetly runs a finger down my arm.

"Ms. McGee if I didn't know any better I'd say you're hitting on me."

"And if I am?" she ponders out loud.

Thankfully a little girl runs up to her, buying me a minute to regain my composure. "Ms. McGee, Julia screamed at me."

With a kind grin, she looks down at her. "And did you tell her you don't like it when she does that?" For a moment the little girl contemplates if she did it or not and when she realizes she didn't Kendall sighs, "Why don't you go talk to her and let her know how you're feeling. It's always best to let others know how you feel."

"Okay!" the little girl screams dramatically and rushes off.

Finally done fixing the swing, I holler out to the children, "All fixed!"

"Thank you Mr. Connor!" they scream at the same time they bum rush the swing in front of me.

Backing up carefully, I head towards the door until Kendall's small soft hand wraps itself around my tattooed forearm. "Wait."

"Yeah?" I glance down at her chipped painted finger nails before I look up to her face. Nothing like the French manicured ones that belong to a girl I can't get out of my head. Damn it. What is my problem?

"Connor, seriously, I was wondering, if maybe you wanted to…" she tries to let her pale Irish skinned hand finish the sentence.

"Maybe…" I nervously run my hand over my black buzz cut hair, "but for now I gotta go."

Doing her best to smile, unsure if she was rejected or not, she stops me once more before I unlock the door. "Hey Connor, I was curious. What does that symbol on your arm mean?"

I glance down at the black mark that was one of the only gifts I got for my 18th birthday. It's a circle connected down the middle with something that looks similar to diamonds, with four smaller circle dots connected to the outer circle wall. One at the top, bottom, and both sides. "To have faith. Belief. Assurance. It's Hawaiian."

"Because you're part—"

"Hawaiian. My father was Hawaiian. Native to the island."

"Why'd he leave?"

"Made the mistake of falling in love with a tourist," the answer is given with an uneasy smile. Talking about my family, especially not the one person who gave a damn in life, isn't something I enjoy.

She giggles, "And MaKayla? You're Hawaiian, so she's part Hawaiian and part…"

"Black. Her mother was black." I swipe my key card. "I'll see you around Kendall."

"Bye cutie." She waves her fingers at me and returns to tugging on her sleeves.

One hot chick is repelled by me, one can't attach herself fast enough. What the hell is wrong with females? Better yet what the hell is wrong with me? The one who would gladly be an asset to my life probably won't pop up in my head again until I see her clocking out for the day. And the other? She won't get out of my head no matter how hard I fucking try.

**

A little past 6:30, when the school is officially closed, I slip my tools back in the work closet and rush to the front office where Nelly is sitting with my daughter in her lap, who is playing with stickers.

"Sorry Nelly, I didn't mean to hold you up." I wipe my hands on my jeans.

"Daddy!" my beautiful daughter, MaKayla, who is almost three years old, rushes into my over worked arms.

"Hi Princess." I hug her tightly and smother her with kisses. She giggles and wiggles in my arms erasing any of the exhaustion I might've just been feeling. Never fails. Love from your daughter can do that. Pulling away I admire her naturally tanned skin, her long black wavy hair that lands directly in the middle of her back, and her glowing green eyes. My daughter is the most beautiful girl in the entire world. I'm thankful she got more of my looks and coloring than her mothers. Makes the pain of what happened a lot easier to fucking swallowing.

"Daddy!" she kisses me again and fiddles with the collar of my shirt. "I miss you!"

"I missed you too." With a wide smile I ask, "Were you being good for Mrs. Nelly?"

She nods sweetly and greets me with the sparkling smile that could melt even the coldest of hearts. "I had a great day Daddy!"

"Did you?" I grab her backpack from Nelly and slide it over my shoulder.

"I did! I finger painted and made you pretty pictures," her small pitched voice squeaks. "In my backpack...I put 'em in my backpack!"

"We'll take them out and put them up in our room when we get home okay?"

"Okay daddy." She drops her head on my shoulder.

I place a kiss on her forehead and whisper to her, "Can you be a good girl and tell Mrs. Nelly goodbye?"

"Bye Mrs. Nelly!" She waves enthusiastically.

"Bye Mak. I'll see you tomorrow okay?" Nelly pushes her fallen blonde strands from her pony tail out of her face, rubs her belly, and smiles.

"Thanks again Nelly for the hand me downs." I try to adjust my daughter on my hip. "They really helped. And the toys...and the--"

She holds up a hand to stop me. "No thanks needed. Glad they are being put to good use rather than collecting dust on my shelf. Can you believe this one is a boy?"

With a slight chuckle, I shrug, "After three girls, I thought you'd be relieved."

"That's one word for it," she lightly jokes. "You two get home. Have a good night."

"You too Nelly."

On our way to the car, Mak squirms around and giggles, clapping her hands while she sings a song I assume she learned today in her preschool class. Loving the sound of her laughter I smile back at her as I unlock my vehicle.

I slide her in the car seat as she continues to sing the song now louder. "You really like that song huh?"

"Love it Daddy!" She claps again, her hair falling into her face. A kiss from her lands on my cheek before she asks, "Can I have Baba please?"

"Of course." I unzip her backpack from next to her and slide her fluffy light brown bear into her hands, which she immediately hugs tightly. With a ruffle of her hair I sigh, "Love you Mak."

Mak squeals in return, "Love you!"

I shut the door and climb into the front seat. With another heavy exhale, fatigue taking over again, I start the car I was lucky to get at the price I did. Damn near cost me everything I had saved when Mak was born, but I try not to complain. The college kid whose parents bought him a brand new car, couldn't seem to get rid of it fast enough. Insurance is cheap enough that I don't feel like I have to break the damn law every time I have to drive her. Pulling out of the parking lot, we head towards home, her favorite princess sing along CD playing. At the first stop light I glance at the clock wondering just how late I'm going to be up tonight doing my calculus homework, writing my English paper and devising a plan to convince Ms. Flores to switch my partner to someone with a more flexible attitude. Though the girl has a pair of very flexible legs. At least they look flexible. In fact I wouldn't mind if they—Mak's voice hits a note so far off key from the song it breaks that train of thought.

Damn it, if I stay up too late Mak wants to stay up with me, which makes it harder for her to get to school on time, which makes it harder for me to get to school on time. While a few of my teachers understand the situation and cut me some slack, it doesn't change the dickhead feeling I get for arriving late sometimes.

The drive home takes twice as long as the drive to work does for the simple fact I live nowhere near the school. In fact I live twenty minutes from the school that I started attending once MaKayla was born. Distance between me and the school I met her mother at seemed best.

We pull into the rundown apartment complex, where the wood looks damp and moldy, the roofs are peeling off, and the metal looks rusty. If those factors aren't appealing enough, then the weeds attacking the parked cars, the overflowing dumpster, and the drug deals possibly being made right out in the open are. Taking the path around to the right, I slowly go over the speed bumps because Mak likes to pretend they are some sort of roller coaster ride, like the ones she's seen on commercials. She always tosses her hands in the air and screams, which breaks my heart. Every time. Saddest part isn't even that I've never been able to take her to any of the places she points out on the T.V., it's the fact that I'll probably never be able to afford to. At least not while she's young. When it matters. The memories I get to make with her are typically at free things, like the park on the better side of town. The same park where parents raise their eyebrows, judging me on my age as a parent just as much as they do on my wardrobe. Just like Gianna did. Ugh. Fuck. Not that girl again. I pull into the space directly in front of my complex, thankfully, and rush to get Mak out due to the cold and random rain that's starting.

With her back pack over one shoulder, mine over the other, her in my arms and the keys in my hand, I hurry up the flight of stairs to the apartment on the right.

"Daddy our number is falling..." Mak points to the 4602 that's dangling for the second time this month. "Fix it."

"Later Mak."

"Now Daddy," she whines.

"No ma'am," I scold her finally getting the keys in the lock.

"But--"

"Daddy said no Mak," I repeat and she starts to pout, which is the last thing I need right now.

As soon as we're inside, I let Mak down and lock all three locks cringing at the idea of having to chase thieves off again.

"Grandma!" Mak screams running towards the couch where my mother is blatantly passed out.

"No, leave Grandma alone baby," I instruct after looking at the empty bottle of Vodka on the coffee table in front of her. "You'll see her in the morning."

"But Daddy," she begins to pout once more, her flawless skin scrunching into tear mode.

"But nothing. You'll see her in the morning."

The whining gets louder, "I wanna see her now."

"Mak, please take your backpack to your room and play with your dolls while I make dinner okay?" My deep sigh is followed by me leaning on the wall beside the front door.

After much hesitation and useless poking at my mother she does as she's asked and drags her backpack to our bedroom. Slipping out of my beat up black shoes, I head across the food and paint stained once white carpet and stare at my mother disappointedly. Like it's not enough she reeks of booze and cigarettes, her legs are wide open leaving that part of her body on display and her head is lifelessly draped off the edge of the couch.

Shaking my head at the image, I'm taken off guard when an unexpected male strolls in the room. Confused, I fold my arms across my broad chest allowing my biceps to bulge in my shirt. Girls think I hit the gym on a regular with some weird goal of looking like a fitness model or something. Fact of the matter is, the work out I get is from work and chasing off scum that tries to stick to my mother.

"And who the fuck are you?" my voice growls.

"Tommy. Who the hell are you?" He pulls his gray shirt over his overly tatted body. Dad had a policy about only getting tattoos that signified something important. Hints to why I have just the one.

"Her son," I answer. "What are you doing here?"

"Her," his laugh creates a familiar knot in my stomach.

My eyes skim over his frail 5'10 structure, his washed out skin, and short shaggy light brown hair. I notice the needle marks in his arm, which never fails to make my skin crawl. Clearing away the anxiety it creates I state, "Well now that you're done, you can go."

"What's that?" He makes a movement towards me in what I'm sure he feels is an intimidating gesture. I've run off drug dealers. Thieves. Crooked landlords. Hundreds of men bigger and more powerful than the wiry guy in front of me, who almost looks like he's going to ask me for chemistry notes.

"I said…" My hands unlocks the door while still making eye contact with him. "You. Can. Go." When I fling the door open I say, "Which means get your shit and get out."

He hesitates at first assuming I'm all talk and no action until he takes note of my defensive stance, which has yet to waiver. I watch as he grabs his brown coat and scuffed up shoes only to quickly exit my apartment, not giving me or my mother a second glance.

Once he disappears, I re-lock the door, swoop all 120 pounds of my mother into my arms and carry her into her bedroom. Kicking a few more beer bottles out of my way, I gently lay her on the bed. Before covering her up with a light purple blanket, one of the only mementos she kept from my father. I make sure to remove her car keys, placing them back in the living room by her purse for work in the morning. The moment I hear a faint snore coming from her, I turn and leave to deal with the other chores that are waiting.

Our bite-sized kitchen is directly across from my mother's bedroom. Sure, the tiny apartment isn't the ideal space except for maybe someone who lives alone, but I've learned to make do. I've learned to cope. As long as Mak has a roof over her head, even if it occasionally leaks, that's all that matters. Crossing towards the direction of the sink, I cringe at the sick remains from what I only hope was food on the floor. Fuck I pray that's food. I drag myself past the sink of overflowing dirty dishes to the fridge and pantry that sit side by side next to the window. Digging through the bare cupboard to see the remains of what can only be described as a food raid, I rub the back of my heavily tensing neck. Frustrated, I quickly move over to admire what's left in the fridge, which ultimately evokes a panged groan out of me. Now when I get paid on Friday I not only have to attempt to pay MaKayla's tuition in full, the light bill, and store away gas money, but restock the kitchen with food that should have lasted another couple of weeks. Looks like God's not about balance, so much as giving me the tiniest light of hope to laugh when I realize it was just a trick.

I rub my tattoo while staring into the basically barren fridge. Faith. Belief. Assurance. Three things that my father would expect me to keep close to me because he did it. Three things that are getting harder to hold onto along-side his principles and fading memory.

I decide to make macaroni and cheese, green beans, and lemon chicken, items obviously no one wants when they have the munchies because it requires too much effort. Slowly, I get everything started at the same time I get the dishes washed. Swinging back by our room, I creak the door open to grab our laundry basket, at the same time Mak is brushing one of her princess dolls' hair. Not being noticed I grab the hamper, so I can begin washing clothes, knowing tomorrow is 'I wanna wear the pink and green polka dot shirt you lied and told me mommy bought last year' Wednesday. I'm just thankful that she only has the one shirt that matters so much to her and that accidents in her underwear are damn near non-existent. Potty training her early saved money I really couldn't waste on pull-ups. Those things are fucking expensive.

As soon as the laundry is going, I return to the living room around the corner to pick up after my mother. For the most part I consider her my other child. At first I take a glance around at the blood smeared wall, the torn apart maroon recliner which has a pile of clean laundry on it, and the wobbly coffee table I have to fix three times a week due to its excessive use for my mother's sexcapades and my daughters frequent coloring. Amazed that no matter how many times I try to tidy the place up, it still manages to appear this way. I take on my cleaning routine again.

The collection of beer bottles and cigarette butts are not only disgusting, but dangerous for Mak to be around. I once saw her lips pressed against an empty bottle because she said she liked the whistling sound it made. Ever since that moment she has never been allowed to play where I haven't cleaned and looked over. Sometimes I wonder if my mother just forgets she's got a baby granddaughter around the place or just doesn't care, but either way someone has to be responsible for the place and it makes the most sense it's me. After throwing away the large amount of drug excess, I do an extra sweep between the couch cushions remembering the one time I found a bottle of pills there. My eyes scan the room once more spotting an empty needle underneath the coffee table. Not sure if I should be more terrified that Mak could have come across this while she was poking at my mother or more pissed off my mother had the nerve to leave it in the living room where Mak could have access to it. I transfer it to the kitchen, put it in a plastic container, and dispose of it in the house trash where I make a mental note to take it to the dumpster the minute MaKayla has fallen asleep.

I vacuum, give the surfaces I know Mak can touch another wipe down, and drag my homework out from my backpack. I spread it out on the floor beside the coffee table so that my daughter may enjoy her coloring session before bed.

"MaKayla," I call to her only to be greeted by her attendance instantly. "Do you wanna watch your favorite movie while we eat dinner?"

"Yes please!" She squeals crawling on the couch behind where I'm sitting, flopping herself and her bear down.

Popping it in the DVD player, which I scored from a garage sale a couple years back, along with the movie, I let her watch the previews she's seen a million times as she giggles helplessly. That sound makes all this shit worth it. The cleaning. The long hours of work. Barely sleeping because of homework. All that is worth it for just one second of that sound.

I return to the kitchen to stir the macaroni around a little bit more just as the chicken has finished baking. With a heartfelt smile on my face, hearing the movie start I grab her princess plate and matching cup along with an adult plate for me. The amazing balancing act I do to carry the plates and her drink into the living room receives another giggle right before she starts to sing along with the first song in the movie. I place the plates down on the coffee table, set up her mini chair so that she may eat at the coffee table, and plop her down in it. Not even really caring she's got dinner in front of her she picks up her fork and begins fighting with the green beans to stay on it while continuing to sing along.

With my own plate to the side of me, I open my calculus book that I swear grows larger every damn day, and begin to do my homework in hopes I can finish in time to go to bed with her.

Chapter 2

6:30 a.m. on the dot, the poking begins. Her tiny toes poke my calf. My hip. Usually a toe tries to find a new home between my ribs. When the beginning efforts of pulling me out of sleep fail, she defaults to her back up plan. Poking me in the arm, the neck, the head, and eventually the ear. Not gonna lie, the ear typically gets me.

I force my eyes open to see her staring at me from a sitting position on top of my chest.

"Daddy," she whines loudly. "Daddy get up! We have to get ready for school!"

"I know," a deep groan escapes me, missing the days where I could sleep in until ten minutes before the bell would ring. Those days are on a long list of things I miss. Decent clothes that fit and an active social life also on that list.

Pushing the hair out of her eyes, I smirk as I relish the fact this little face that greets me every morning caught most of my genetics. I couldn't handle the heartbreak of waking up to her mother's face every morning. "Good morning."

"Morning Daddy!" another adorable giggle leaves her. I have to be the world's luckiest dad to have a daughter with such an even temperament.

"Did my angel sleep well?"

"Yes. Did Daddy?"

"Yes. Thanks for asking," I sit slightly up, her knees digging into my exposed six pack. "Do you want a bagel for breakfast?"

"Cereal."

"You had cereal yesterday. How about a little bit of yogurt and a bagel?"

"Cereal."

"How about a few grapes and toast?"

She folds her arms over her favorite princess nightgown in protest. "Cereal."

Rolling my eyes, ready to fight with her like I do at least twice a week in the morning, I'm interrupted by my mother who's out of her drunken state and has ventured into her hang over mode.

"Oh let the child have some damn cereal," she sighs hitting the light, which stings my eyes.

"Grandma!" Mak springs off my chest and our queen sized bed into my mother's arm.

"Hello baby." My mother holds her tight before Mak begins to try to pull the curls out she just put in. "You being a good girl for daddy?"

"Yes." Mak lays her head on her shoulder. "But I want cereal."

"I know." She places a kiss on her forehead. "I'll take you to the kitchen and make you a bowl. You can eat while I have my coffee and Daddy gets his lazy butt out of bed to take a shower. Sound good?"

Lazy? Which one of us busts their ass to go to school and work, to take care of their child? Which one of us cleans the house and does the laundry while the other one gets drunk and whores them self around? If that is the definition of lazy, I might need to start using a dictionary to clarify simple words.

"Yes!" she squeals for glee as they exit out of the room.

I lay my head back down on my pillow for a second hoping to get another moment of sleep since it's rare. She can have four bowls of cereal if I can have just another five minutes.

"Shower now, Connor!" My mother's shrill voice screeches from the kitchen.

"I'm going!" I yell back slowly hauling myself out of the bed and into the bathroom directly next to our bedroom.

In general, my shower time has been extended a little longer each day Mak gets older. On rare days like today when my mother is up earlier than expected, she helps get her dressed and hair fixed. While Mak doesn't appreciate the simplicity of having her hair brushed and a colorful hair band added, I am quite proud of what I've learned to do. My mother taught me in the beginning how much easier her hair would be to deal with when it was wet. To always wet the brush or comb first. Be slow and gentle and distract during the tangles. It's almost amazing to think about how loving she is when she's not guzzling booze. Or offering what lies between her legs for a less than adequate price. After my brief ten minute shower, which is just enough time to wake up, scrub myself off, and wash my hair, I quickly stumble back into my room to slide into a pair of jeans I find, a baby blue t-shirt with a dark blue button down shirt on top. On the way back to the bathroom, I run my fingers over my hair to shake away any access water. In an odd multitasking combination, I start brushing my teeth and fastening my belt at the same time.

"Daddy! Daddy! Look!" Mak comes bouncing into the bathroom wearing the shirt I specifically washed yesterday, jeans, pink tennis shoes, and a pair of high pigtails.

Spitting out the toothpaste, I quickly rinse my mouth out, before exclaiming, "Oh! Nice pig tails. Did Grandma do those for you?"

"Yes..." She wiggles back and forth, her baba in her hand.

"Well how about you go get your backpack, so I can take you to school?"

"But I want Grandma to take me to school."

"Grandma has to get to work," I remind her only to see her bottom lip start to poke out.

"But Daddy—"

"MaKayla Ashley..."

"Fine," her voice croaks before she stomps away. I fucking hate being the only parent. The only one who has to tell her no. The only one to share the responsibility of having to explain to her why certain things can't happen, like attending her friends' birthday parties.

When I exit the bathroom I run straight into my mother who is dressed and ready for work. Last night she looked like a stripper in her black mini skirt, gold bathing suit top, yet now she looks the professional banker she pretends to be during the day. She's a supervisor of a bank downtown in which she has to carry herself like she's in corporate America, but at night after a long days' work of pretending to be stable she lets loose by being the town slut.

"Mom, I know you like to drink especially when you get off--"

"Of course I do."

"And I'm not asking you not to--"

"Which is good because I would tell you to fu-"

"I'm asking, could you refrain from leaving the bottles around the house?"

"They're just bottles Connor."

Still whispering under my breath I add, "Not to mention the drug products--"

24

"Don't talk to me like that," she snaps while buttoning down her black business jacket. "This is my household, and I'll do as I damn well please."

"Your household?" I'm taken off guard as I watch her pull down her matching pencil skirt. "Your household?"

"I pay the rent don't I?"

"Barely. And that's about all you pay."

"Don't start Connor." She disapprovingly shakes her finger at me.

"You know Mom, I could care less if you wanna get drunk day in and day out, but think about MaKayla okay? I've caught her with a bottle before that still had alcohol in it. Not to mention I hate for her to see her grandmother passed out like a drunken whore on the couch."

"How dare you..." her voice trembles.

"Oh don't even." I shake my head and walk around her to grab my backpack from my bedroom. Lord knows I'm going to have enough theatrics in my day already. At least the other one comes on a pair of legs I swear I've only seen on Victoria Secret Angel models.

"You know what Connor? I don't feel like dealing with your bullshit this morning!" She screams at me not realizing Mak is behind her.

"Language please." My head nods in Mak's direction, who looks like she might cry, much like she always does when she hears us fighting.

"Sorry," she apologizes to my daughter, leans down and kisses her on the forehead. "Can you go sit on the couch while Grandma and Daddy finish talking please?" She nods and slowly wanders off towards the direction of the living room. My mother shuts my door after her to return to yelling, "Who the hell do you think you are? I am the mother and you are the child."

"No I am a father and that is my child." I point the direction my daughter went. "You hardly classify as a mother half the time."

"I put a roof over your head—"

"No, the men you sleep with put the roof over my head, but then again you're right mom. Someone has to sleep with them in order for that money to pay rent."

25

Her fingers violently run through her bobbed, dyed blonde hair, a color my father hated on her. "You think that's funny Connor?"

"Do you see me laughing? You think I enjoy the fact my mother is the town tramp? It's not exactly something I'm going around bragging about."

"I do what I want on my own time! You never hear me complain about your personal life!"

"What personal life?!" I snap. "How the hell can I have a personal life between caring for you when you're drunkenly passed out and watching for drugs around the house I don't want my child to get into. Oh, not to mention the strange men that randomly appear in the apartment. Can't forget to add making sure they don't try to pound my face in or rob us. How can I possibly have a personal life when I spend every waking moment taking care of other people?"

"Connor—"

"I'm not even listening." I raise a hand. "I just wanted to make a point to let you know that I'm sick of seeing your drugs or your boyfriend's drugs or whoever's drugs around the house, so if could please just try to keep it in your room so that my 2½ almost 3 year old doesn't get a hold of them that would be really appreciated."

She pouts her pink glossed lips at me before she tosses her hands in the air to surrender. For a moment she stares at me, one hand wrapped around her stomach and the other pressed against her heart as if it aches. This isn't the life she expected to live. Hell this isn't the life either of us expected to fall into.

"If you'll excuse me, I have to get my daughter to school." I open the door and stroll out past her with a fake smile on my face in hopes of confusing MaKayla, who's camped out with her coloring book. "Come on Mak. It's time to go."

MaKayla slides off the couch and over to me so that I can button her light jacket and her pink puffy marshmallow coat.

Fighting tears my mother whispers, "Button her up tight okay babe?"

Without so much as glancing her direction, I sigh, "Will do."

Once she's snug, I join her by sliding on my black oversized leather jacket I was sent from my grandmother for Christmas, over my outfit. She was my father's mother. Still lives in Hawaii. She sends me extra money when she gets a chance or hand me down clothes from a neighbor. She's even offered to have me and Mak pack up our entire lives and move there to live with her and my grandfather. To live the way my dad would've wanted. More secure. Safe. Peaceful.

Prepared to leave it unzipped my mother calls out again, "You too. It's cold outside."

My shoulders slump slightly as I turn around to face her, mascara drops on her cheek, trembling hands fumbling around for a place to land on her body, and wobbly legs doing their best to stand strong. There used to be a time when she wasn't weak. I guess this is the echo death leaves.

Instinctively I cross the room, wrap my arms around her, and whisper sweetly, "It'll be okay Mom. It always is."

Pulling away she nods, touches my cheek, and tries to smile. She lets me go and calls to her granddaughter, "Have a good day Princess, okay? Play nice with everyone."

"I will," Mak giggles her pigtails bouncing back and forth. "Thank you for my piggy tails."

"You're welcome. Grandma loves you."

"I love you too." She blows my mother a kiss and tries to reach the door knob.

"And I love you." My mother's hand lands on my shoulder before gently touching my chin. The pain I can see running through her eyes because I look like my father makes me even more grateful Mak doesn't look like her mother. Clearly trying to shake off the emotions, she pulls back and folds her arms across her chest, "Be careful."

I briefly nod before strolling away to pick up MaKayla, our backpacks, and take off towards my car in the violently, cold wind.

Hours later after being late to first period again and suffering through a long day of Calculus, a subject I highly doubt I'll ever need, and econ, where my teacher is obsessed with old 80s videos he thinks we can learn from, I'm fortunate enough to be sitting at a lunch table with my two best friends. More like my only friends. By choice. The less people I have poking around in what goes on when I leave campus, the better. Our conversations are usually about video games, something I rarely get to play, but more often now that I got a used X-box 360, which I keep hidden in my room. While Brent and I skipped school to get me a tat for my birthday, Bret gave me his old system he was going to sell back to the game store, claiming he was so tired of me not having a clue what the hell they were talking about. Looks like pity, feels like pity, but it's friendship. Long before they knew anything about my secret most people could never guess, they were still my friends. Friends from the moment, I put them in their place on the basketball court. Hey, I may have had to leave the team behind at my other school, but it doesn't mean I have to leave the skills there too.

Unfortunately for me, only a few minutes into the conversation, the pair of legs for days with the mouth made for misery, comes waltzing over to the table.

"Connor," Gianna speaks with a manipulative smirk.

Not responding, I continue with my conversation, "Wait, so what happens when you make it to the part where he—"

"Connor," she interrupts once more.

Doing my best to hide my growing annoyance, I try again, "The part where he—"

"Connor," she pouts louder this time, grabbing my friend's attention like she's some sort of foreign goddess. Fine. Between the coffee colored legs, the short skirt, the knee high leather boots, and the incredible tight white sweater, she looks good. Damn good. Almost good enough to forget the fact that her high horse is on the top of a fucking mountain.

I place another chip in my mouth, the small amount of lunch I can afford.

Gianna snaps, "Aren't you going to say hi?"

"Hadn't planned on it," my answer makes my two friends snicker.

Slightly riled she huffs, "Aren't you going to introduce me to your friends?"

With a completely serious face I question, "And why would I ever do such a thing?"

"Ugh," her growl turns into another pout as she folds her arms across her chest. After a moment she whines again, "Well…"

"Well…what?"

"Introduce me."

"I don't want to."

"Come on."

"No."

"Just introduce me." She stomps her boot covered foot at me.

"No." I land another chip in my mouth.

"Yes."

"No."

"Yes."

"No." Our conversation gains more chuckles from my friends.

Gianna slightly leans over and whispers in my ear. "Introduce me before I introduce myself in a way that'll get the whole school talking about you."

Not sure if her threat holds any ground, but not willing to risk my good name being challenged, I sigh, "Brent and Bret, this is Gianna." She smiles widely at the two of them as they ogle her decent rack. A weird surge of jealousy shoots through me. Quickly I dismiss it by declaring, "She's a stripper."

Her jaw hits the ground and before she can snap back Bret playfully asks, "Really? I was hoping to get one for my 18th birthday. Do you think you could help me out? Give us a discount?"

Clearing her throat, she pops her hip to the side and smirks, "Boys, could you please excuse us? I have something I need to talk to the last resort about."

The two of them look at me for approval of dismissal. Once received, they pick up their trash and allow Gianna to sit down at the lunch table across from me.

"Can I help you?" I ask in an all too familiar tone to her. "Was being a bitch yesterday not enough to last you a couple days? Do you have to hit the restart button every morning when you wake up?"

"Look Connor, I know yesterday we got off on the wrong foot—"

"Wrong foot? That's putting it mildly."

"Fine. Yesterday we got off to a bad start—"

"Bad start? My car gets off to a bad start on a cold morning."

"Fine awful. Whatever. I'd just like to say I'm not a bad person—"

"Said the devil right before God kicked him out."

"I mean I'm really not so terrible once you get to know me—"

"Is what a serial killer says in court right before they're about to sentence him."

"In fact if you just give me a chance I'm sure—"

"I'll hate you more as time goes on."

"Damn it! Will you let me talk?!"

"Why?"

"Because I'm trying to apologize!"

"Are you?"

"Yes."

"Are you really?"

"Yes!"

"And why is that?" I admire the frustrated look on her skillfully painted face. Even though I hesitate to admit this, but evil never looked so beautiful. There's something about the simplicity of her make up that doesn't distract from her hazel eyes, her high cheek bones, or the dimple that slightly exists in her left cheek.

"Because I wanna be your partner."

"Uh-huh and why's that?"

"Because I think you've got real potential," she says in what sounds like a rehearsed tone. I give her an emotionless stare. "Because I think you've got real talent." Not receiving a different response with that she tries to keep muttering responses she thinks I want to hear, "Because you're amazing. Because everyone wants to be your partner. Because—"

"They called you in the office didn't they?" A slight grin of triumph covers my face.

"Ugh yes. God, I didn't know how much more I could keep that lying up," she sighs pulling out a bottle of water from her purse. "They hadn't called me in the office in almost a week. You don't think I know why I got a request there today?" She says in what sounds like an upset tone. "Now look, I know I wasn't very nice to you yesterday, so I came to say I'm sorry." My continued blank stare is followed with, "I really do want to be your partner."

"No you don't."

"Yes I do."

"No you don't. What you should say is you really don't want them to kick you out of school."

"Isn't that what I said?"

"You're unbelievable." I shake my head and get up.

"Thank you!" Her marvelous smile graces my presence before she gets up to follow me over to the trash can. If only she wasn't so damn sexy, it would be easier not to be tempted by that smile. The all charming, she knows she's hot shit smile. She may be hot shit, but I'm not that dumb. Not dumb enough to fall for a gorgeous face and tiny waist. Well, at least not twice.

"That wasn't a compliment," I mumble underneath my breath tossing my trash away and heading towards the theater room.

"Wait!" She rushes to catch up with me, her boots tapping loudly. "Connor wait!"

Past the point of annoyed I whip around, "What? What do you want from me Gianna?"

"To give me another chance."

"And why should I? Because you so kindly welcomed me with open arms? Or because you so sweetly dismissed the only peace I experience during the day? Why should I waste another moment of my precious, and I do mean precious, time listening to bullshit from you when you looked down your nose at me to begin with?"

"Because I'm desperate!" She pleads, her eyes on the brink of tears, though I'm fairly certain they're not real.

"Honesty. Nice. I appreciate that, but that doesn't sound like my problem." My eyes invite themselves to leisurely roll over her small curves, tight stomach, and down the most dangerous set of legs in existence. Those should be registered as deadly weapons.

Gianna pulls me into the hallway by the hand and pushes me against the wall. The slight action feels like foreplay. I have to use will power to force my dick to stay down. "Look, if I don't make this work with you that's it for me."

Heartlessly, I draw a set of fake tears down my cheeks, which boils her.

"I don't think you understand."

"I don't think I care."

"Boarding school is just like Juvy! Both are only full of girls and reek of bad endings."

I sigh teasingly, "Tick-tock..."

"Look, I don't want to leave another school especially because I slipped up and wouldn't let what seems like…" she delays the next part as if choking on it, "…an actual decent person have a chance. Now, I know you want to win that competition for whatever reason, so if you let yesterday's episode go and give us a fresh start today and tell Ms. Flores you've changed your mind, I promise to take this seriously."

"Promise huh?" The back of my head rests against the wall. "Can I get that in blood?"

Clearly biting her tongue she moves past my snide remark. "I swear. I'll be serious every step of the way and really put something into this."

"Do you even have something to put into this? I mean how do I know you've even got potential? How do I know I'm not working with another every day girl who thinks because she reads her poems on YouTube to a handful of followers, she's gonna be the next big thing?"

"You've gotta trust me."

"That sounds like a very bad idea."

"I'm throwing up my white flag here. Whatever you need me to do for this competition I will. I will do whatever it takes, whenever it takes. Whatever you say goes for this project, just please, please, don't let them send me away again," her plea does something that I've got to learn to control. It strikes guilt in my heart. It reminds me of an all too familiar tale I once got, which is in the end how I got stuck as a single parent.

"Fine," my groan is deep and pained. "One more chance, but I swear to God Gianna if you so much as make one comment or smart ass remark I don't like that's it. You can kiss the easy public school life goodbye and prepare yourself to hug the 'I'm desperately dying for a make-over before I become an angry lesbian' boarding school hello. We clear?"

"Like a high quality diamond engagement ring." She winks.

Why the hell am I such a sap for girl with a sob story? You'd think I'd learn after MaKayla that sometimes it's best to just let the troubled ones go, but no. Who am I kidding? I know why I'm like this. His view of life, determination to never stop seeing the good in the bad, pumps through my veins just as his DNA does. On days like today, I wish I was nothing like him. It would significantly decrease the chances of my life falling apart.

Chapter 3

A couple days later, I'm stretching my legs out in front of me, just as Nicole Simon, a girl I've had every theater class with since I started at this school, leans over to whisper, "How are things with Tyra Banks' evil twin?"

I glance back to see Gianna looking down at us with a slightly disapproving look. With a snicker I merely shake my head and turn back around.

"She's death glaring me again isn't she?" I nod. "That girl has to work for the devil. Maybe his assistant?"

Sarcastically I tilt my head, "Do you really see that Pretty Pretty Princess working for anyone else?"

She giggles and playfully touches my arm. "Get this though. I heard from Carly who sits behind her in English, that she was doodling your initials."

"Do you know how many people have my initials?"

"Okay. But how many people are willing to have anything to do with her?"

With that point made, I glance over my shoulder again to see Gianna quickly look away, to hide the fact she was obviously still staring. Concerned that Nicole is right I turn back around just as Ms. Flores takes the front of the classroom.

"Now let's look at today's rotation," Ms. Flores says with excitement.

She starts listing the spaces outside of the classroom that we have share on a cycle, announcing at the end it's me and Gianna's turn in the auditorium. All that space and nothing to do with it yet.

Getting up, I grab my backpack and walk from my bottom row seat to the door where I lean my back against it. I watch my partner who takes her dear sweet time to do everything like the world revolves around her. My foot taps the ground impatiently as she swishes her hips, which are covered with another mini skirt, leather this time, down the stairs while the entire class watches, myself included. Every time she walks I swear she's strutting down a runaway. It's like she was made to grab the attention of everyone effortlessly. Frustrated that I can't shake the attraction and the fact she's making me wait in front an audience, I move out of the door way when she finally gets close enough letting the door close in her face. Hearing the class chuckle serves as sufficient payback.

"Well that wasn't very nice," she snaps rushing to follow me down the hallway towards the stage.

"Yeah and neither is making me wait thirty minutes for you to walk from the top of the stairs to the bottom like you're some sort of super model or something."

"I was," she mumbles adjusting her shoulder bag.

"What?"

"Nothing." Her throat clears as she finally catches up to me. "Sorry. I'm just used to walking and it not mattering."

"Well it does now," I snap, opening the door to the stage, ushering her through. "We need every bit of rehearsal time in class we can get."

"Yeah I meant to talk to you about that." Gianna sets her bag by the door and adjusts her sweater that's letting her belly button ring play peak-a-boo with me. The little yellow gem catches my eye again and suddenly I wish my fingertips were touching it.

Pulling my script out of my backpack, I try to keep my eyes diverted to shake off the thought. Shoving my bag to the side, I flop down on one of the stage couches. These things have seen more action than Prom Night. Or so I assume. I didn't get to go to my junior prom. Not going to my senior one either. "About what?"

"This whole rehearse only in class thing. From what I hear everyone else practices outside of school. And according to Ms. Flores it's something she recommends."

I do my best to focus on my highlighted lines and not on what she's saying, "Well we don't. We work in class."

"What about outside? Like after school?"

"I get out of school at 2:00."

"Perfect! So do I," her excitement feels genuine as she bounces down on the purple couch cushion next to me. One minute it feels like she's determined to say everything she can to hurt me and the next it's like she wants someone to talk to. Whiplash isn't something I wanna add to my life. I swear...chicks.

"Not perfect. I have to be at work by 2:30."

"You have a job?"

"Some of us can't have Mommy and Daddy give us everything."

The snip causes her to glare. "What about after work?"

"I have other responsibilities to take care of."

"Like what?"

"Like," the words are ready to rush out of my mouth just to get her off my back when the obvious shuts me up.

Very few know about MaKayla, which is a Goddamn miracle. Keeping her birth off social media was a challenge, but when you have someone who doesn't want the world to know any more than you do, it gets a little easier. However there are a few teachers who bend the rules for me. Bret and Brent who try to help in subtle ways, like grabbing too many slices of pizza on days it's clear I can't afford to eat. The preschool I work at donates used things to me when they get brand new ones to keep their school looking the best of the best or ahead of the rest. It's this combination of generosity that no one can see that even gives me a shot at raising Mak as successfully as I have. No one else needs to know. I don't need those questions. I don't want that attention.

"Like things that aren't any of your concern. Can we get started now?"

"No," she protests again, leaning up against the couch arm of the hideous flowered couch. "What kind of things?"

"Things."

"Like?"

"Like I said."

"How do you expect me to put 'everything' into this if you aren't?" Gianna tilts her chin down with another disapproving glare.

Getting underneath my skin, which is becoming a usual for her, I dig my fingers into the couch. "I am putting my everything into it, but I have some stipulations on my time. Therefore, we have to work in class and in class only."

"Why does the world have to be all about *you*?"

"Why does the world have to be all about *you*?"

"You're being difficult."

"You are difficult..."

"Fine! I give up!" She throws her hands up in submission. "Whatever."

"Can we start now?"

Gianna shrugs and crosses her legs. "Sure."

"Let's take it from page 7," I sigh.

For a moment it's silent as I try to review my lines over and over again in my head, determined to find my character's voice, when Gianna interrupts with, "Do you have a girlfriend?"

"What?" my concentration breaks to look up at her.

"Do you have a girlfriend?" She innocently nibbles on the edge of her fingernail. My eyes drift to the action, my imagination rushing to get away from me.

"Why?"

"Because that's the only excuse I can think of as being 'other responsibilities'."

"The only excuse?"

"Yeah…"

"Wow."

"Wow what?"

"You really are just a simple creature aren't you?"

With another shrug she asks, "So, do you?"

"No." I bury my face back in my script.

"She's probably another theater nerd isn't she?"

"I just said no. No girlfriend. Can we get back to lines now?"

"I guess," another huff escapes her. As soon as I open my mouth to say my first line she blurts, "Why not?"

Irritated I gripe, "Why not what?"

"Why don't you have a girlfriend?"

"I don't know. I just…don't," my answer is nowhere near truthful. I know exactly why I don't have a girlfriend. I know exactly why I keep my space away from females. And MaKayla's beautiful face acts as the perfect reminder when I threaten to get a little too close to one.

"You just don't?"

"That's what I said."

"You mean to tell me a guy like you can't get a girlfriend? That doesn't make sense."

"I didn't say I can't get a girlfriend. I said I don't have a girlfriend."

"Tomato…potato." She waves her hand at me in dismissal.

"No, there's a big difference between can't and don't. I can have a girlfriend. Hell, I've had numerous amounts of girls chasing me since I first came to this school and I CHOOSE not to have a girlfriend."

37

"Player type? Enjoy the run around?"

"Not at all actually," my heavy sigh is followed by hands running over my buzz cut. "I prefer the idea of just one girl. One girl that I don't have to share. One girl that...that I can call my own."

"Chump."

Offended I bite, "Excuse me?"

"I didn't say anything," she mumbles before she begins to admire her nails.

"You did, and I wanna know what you mean by that."

"By what? That you're a chump? Because I thought the definition of that word was pretty clear."

I get off the couch and prepare to head towards the door. "You know what, between the twenty question and twenty insults, I just don't think that this is going to work out. I'm just going to tell Ms. Flores that—"

"Whoa whoa whoa there cowboy," she wraps her surprisingly soft and warm hands around my forearm before I have the chance to walk completely by. Something causes her to stutter, "I-I-I didn't mean to offend you."

"Yes you did."

"I really didn't. Swear. It's just...I'm not real good at this whole...friendship thing."

"Apparently." Shaking loose her hand from me I question, "And who said anything about needing a friendship? This is a partnership for business. Think about it like that."

"And as a partnership for a business, it is important to not only know your clients, which in this case would be our audience, but to know my colleague or personal investor. As a good business move it's wise to often take your fellow partner out for lunch and get to know them on a personal level. In the end you'll understand them better on the business front and be better aware of where they'll be going with their ideas."

Seeing exactly where she's coming from, I sigh, "And how do you know all this?"

"Daddy's got a lot of businesses." She nods slowly. "A lot." In a soft whisper she adds, "So many it makes it easy for him to forget he has me..." A surge of guilt shoots through me forcing me to open my mouth to say something when she proceeds, "Anyway, I've just never been good at the whole friendly speech thing. I really haven't had many…"

"Speeches or friends?"

Sensing the playfulness in my tone she smirks. "Friends."

"But you have met people before right?" my body slides on to the arm of the couch beside her.

"Not your kind of people."

"And what the hell is that supposed to mean?"

Nervous at the subject, she reaches in her purse to fidget for something. "Nothing. Never mind."

My hand covers her cellphone screen. "You know what Gianna? I'm sick of all these questions you demand I answer yet when I ask you something that is the end of the conversation. From now on if you want answers you're going to have to cough them up too, otherwise just leave it the fuck alone. Deal?"

"Deal." She gently nudges my hand off her screen. After a short pause she says, "I just find it odd for a guy like you not to have a girlfriend for whatever reason."

"What's that supposed to mean? A guy like me?"

Gianna pops off the couch, slides by me, and shrugs. "Nothing. Never mind."

Watching her head back to her backpack, allowing a beautiful shot of her ass that's trying to peak at me from underneath the skirt, I find myself boiling with irritation not only with her damn questions but that this is some sick twist of my physical patience as much mental. How am I not supposed to wonder what's under that skirt? Her boots conspire with her legs to point your attention there! Adjusting my jeans, I turn to the side to hide the evidence better. "What do you mean?"

"Nothing," she bends over. You've got to be shitting me. My eyes shoot away to look at the bright stage lightening. "Nothing at all."

"Liar."

"Excuse me?"

"Did I stutter?"

With a heavy sigh she shakes her head. "Whatever. I didn't wanna tell you anyway."

Getting up now that my dick has given up on the idea of what used to happen when a girl would bend over like that, I head over to where she is. "Sure you did. That's why you brought it up. Because you want me to drag answers out of you. Because you want all my attention on you. You're really not that clever Gianna."

"Call me Gi," the correction is accompanied with a cocoa lip gloss being glazed on her lips. Great now, she doesn't just look as good as chocolate she fucking smells like it too. Unbelievable.

"What?"

"Call me Gi. Everyone calls me Gi."

"And by everyone you mean…your followers in hell?"

"No I mean my…" her voice trails off as she realizes she doesn't have friends or if so she doesn't have contact with them. For her sake I'm hoping it's not the latter.

Like a good guy who hates to see a woman suffer, I sigh, "You're name's Gianna."

"Yeah, but my nickname's Gi."

A chuckle escapes me, "Special."

"It is special. You know, Gi, like in G –spot." One of her fingers lightly strolls down my chest. My body's immediate response is to tense from the action while my dick knocks against my jeans again. Damn it! This girl has to be an assistant to the devil and on her agenda today? Turn my nuts blue.

I take a moment and stare into her deep hazel eyes, wondering why she plays so many games. One moment she's being a complete and total bitch and the next she's trying to flirt with me. I fell for those kinds of games once. Never again.

With a wide grin she sneers at me, "Or maybe you don't. Not all guys are capable of finding it ya know?"

Right as she begins to flounce off again further continuing this game of cat and mouse, I grab her by the wrist and spin her around so her back hits the wall and I'm in front of her. "First of all, don't be mistaken…I do know where that spot is." Not loosening my grip, but tightening it, I lean my lips down to her ear that's got two piercings and one in the cartilage. In a heated whisper I say, "Trust me."

A whimper escapes her lips. I lean back to look into her eyes. Her body language is screaming at me to kiss her. The way her eyes are lit up. The way she's holding her breath. And now, her bottom lip being sucked into her mouth demonstrating where she wants tongue.

Steadying myself I let go and insist, "Now tell me, Gi, what you meant."

Gianna swallows deeply, slightly wets her lips and props her foot against the wall. With a flick of her dark brown hair out of her face she answers, "I meant that a guy who is…built with a great body like yours, and green eyes to die for, and a smile that turns knees into jelly, should have a girlfriend. I meant there's no reason for a guy who's caring and forgiving and smart and funny to not have a girlfriend."

My face leans back down into hers. "And how do you know I'm all those things?"

She fiddles around with the edge of her shirt. "I don't. I was making an educated guess. The truth is I don't know you or anything about you."

I let my lips reach her ear once more, "Exactly."

With that said, I turn around and head back to the couch, which is when I hear her mumble, "But I would definitely like to."

"What'd you say?" I pretend to have not heard her as I flop down on the couch once more.

"Nothing…" she denies strolling back over to me. "Where were we?"

Quickly I answer, "Page seven. And let's try to get these lines down so we can actually work on other things next class. Like blocking."

Gianna gives me one final look that raises all sorts of red flags to me. I couldn't date her even if she did more than just push my buttons. I can't date. It's just not something I can do. Not for a very long time. Damn though. This girl is definitely tempting. Even if it's just to…no. Definitely not that. One kid is enough. Gianna looks down and starts flipping around in her script. Maybe we will actually get something accomplished today other than the headache I feel coming on.

Chapter 4

Once I'm finally at work I do my best to try to take it easy knowing all the stress from school could probably just cause me to break things rather than fix them. I don't know what it is about that girl, but there's something I just can't stay away from. It's more than just being horny or really horny in my case. It's like a nagging to see why she's so defensive. Huh. My dad would say that's a higher power's way of telling you to take that path. Gianna is not a path I wanna take. I have enough hoops, hurdles, and hard times without adding one gorgeous misunderstood female to it.

While wandering around I make sure to pass by MaKayla's classroom to see her playing cheerfully with her two best friends, Claire and Zoë, who I need to make sure to invite to her birthday party. It won't be anything huge, but I've been saving to at least do something this year. Hell, I'll see if I can grab some yard work favors to make sure she gets to have some sort of celebration she'll enjoy. Right as I walk away, I hear a call of distress for an overflowing toilet in Ms. Kendall's Pre-K class.

Entering with the mop bucket and plunger, the kids take their attention away from playing and direct it at me.

"Mr. Connor! Mr. Connor!" they squeal trying to rush to me, but are stopped by Kendall and her assistant, who quickly insists that they return to playing.

Within a matter of moments they're gone and Kendall says to me, "I'll show you, which toilet it is." Following behind her, my eyes get a brief glance at her ass in her work pants, not feeling even slightly impressed. Not after seeing Gianna bent over today. Ugh. Damn it! Again? What is she, some sort of voodoo priestess? I haven't consistently thought about a female like this since before Mak was born. Kendall opens the girl's bathroom door, points, and smiles. "All yours Mr. Fix-It."

A chortle escapes me as I tend to the mess. "Thanks."

"Any time," she jokes leaning against the door frame with her eyes glancing at the children. After a moment of silence she asks, "How are you today?"

"I'm alright," I reply. Better if I could get one super model sexy girl out of my fucking head. "You?"

"Great now that I've seen your face," her flirtation grabs my attention.

Doing my best to unclog the toilet, I shake my head, "You're too sweet Kendall."

"I try." She tosses her bangs out of her eyes. "Am I sweet enough to have a date with?"

Taken off guard, I let the plunger slip in my hands. "What?"

Her eyes continue to watch her children, but her voice stays directed at me, "Well, I was just wondering if maybe when you got off if you'd wanna have dinner together or something?"

"I um… have to take Mak home and get her fed and to bed," I regain my composure.

"She can come too," she quickly says. "I love kids, obviously. So I would love if she came with us."

"I don't know Kendall…"

"Oh come on Connor," her voice begins a pout. "I'm dying to spend time with you outside of this place."

Thankful the toilet is finally fixed I begin mopping. "And why is that?"

"Isn't it obvious?" Kendall pushes the hair out of her eyes again and gives me an innocent glance. "I like you Connor."

"You barely know me," my huff is followed by the sound of the mop hitting the water. Which at this point is the truth for all women outside a selected few for me. No one is allowed to know me. Besides, there's nothing more to know about me than I'm an 18 year old single fucking father.

"Well I like what I know," she argues and lets her shoulders shrug. "And want to know more." After another awkward pause she sighs, "Do you…like me?"

Rolling the mop out of the bathroom I give a deep look into her bright blue eyes. "I barely know you." I notice the disappointed look on her face and mutter, "But what I know I like."

Satisfied she waves to me as I exit hoping that's the last time I have to deal with that sort of awkward situation. This day just keeps getting better and better.

Hours later I pick up my daughter slightly earlier than expected, which leaves just enough time to grab dinner on our way home, a rare opportunity.

I hold MaKayla's hand and the Pete's pizza box while both backpacks beat up my back during our travel up the apartment stairs. Before we even reach the faded blue door I hear vicious yelling that makes the blood in my veins begin to boil.

Glancing down at Mak whose face now looks slightly terrified, I instruct her, "Go straight to your room and close the door tight until Daddy comes to get you okay?"

"Yes Daddy." She nods tightening her grip on her teddy bear.

As soon as I open the door she darts down the hall to our room having done this many times before. My attention quickly diverts to my mother's lover, the man she likes to call my stepfather, as his pale rough hands twist around her neck while she struggles to breathe against the wall.

Dropping the backpacks and pizza, I rush over to the toothpick size, balding man and yank him off of her in one quick motion. Without hesitation he swings his fist, which lands directly on my jaw. Not getting a second to process that thought, another swing comes my way, but instead of damaging my face for a second time, it's blocked. Quickly I grab his arm and twist it around his back. I pin him up against the wall, unfortunately inhaling the bitter smell of whiskey.

My face leans over to look into his cocaine glazed eyes, "What the hell are you doing? How many times have I told you not to come around here?"

"And how many times did I try to teach your punk ass to duck when you see a fist coming at you?" He laughs again. "Yet, you still manage to get sucker punched."

Shoving him into the wall again, he grunts, and I respond, "I'm going to ask you again. What the hell are you doing here?"

"It's the first. Rent is due, and you know that tramp you call your mother needs giving and I need getting." This time I grip his hair with my other hand shove his head violently into the wall. After another groan of pain he mutters, "What's wrong Junior? Don't like knowing what a slut Mommy is?"

My grip tightens to the point of bruising. "My mother is—"

"Open like 7-11."

With one more vicious shove of his head into the wall I state, "My mother does what she feels she has to do to pay bills, but she isn't your personal punching bag."

"Why not? My fist fits so sweetly in her jaw," the disturbing tone returns to his voice.

I turn him around, shove him again, this time with my forearm jammed in his throat. "I want you to get your shit and get the hell out. And if I catch you around here ever again you'll need an oxygen tank to breathe. If I decide you get to keep breathing."

"Ha," Paul manages to grunt through my choking. "You don't have it in you."

My eyebrows lower as my eyes glare into his. "Test me."

Our eyes dangerously linger, rage of two different rivers flowing swiftly against each other creating a rapid of tension in which only one of us can survive.

Shoving my arm away he shrugs and looks at my mother, "I'm out of here Lily."

With her hand on her swollen face she rushes towards him, "Paul I—"

"See you on the first of next month." He snatches his leather jacket off the couch.

Paul winks at me, slams the front door, and my mother suddenly breaks into tears chasing after him, "Come back!" In one clean motion, she's in my grip kicking and screaming, "Paul!"

"Stop!" She continues struggling.

"Paul!!"

When her tantrum starts to dwindle, I loosen my hold. "He's gone Mom." Letting her go completely, I lock the door and pick up the pizza box, trying to ignore the pain throbbing in my jaw.

With tears staining her cheek she cries out, "I hate you!"

Nodding, I move the pizza box to the coffee table, replacing the empty whiskey, vodka, and beer bottles. I shake my head gathering the cocaine tray and razor.

"I hate you Connor!" her repeating high pitch scream is a sound both I and the neighbors are accustomed too. "I hate you so much! You're the world's worst son!"

"Funny coming from the world's worst mother," I mumble hiding the mess in the kitchen.

"Why'd you do that? Why'd you throw him out?" she screams, stomping around like my two and half year old. Dropping the bottles in the trashcan I grab the cleaning wipes and stroll back into the living room. "Why? Why? Why!"

45

"Because he's a pot dealing, coke sniffing, womanizing bastard who hits you!"

"He doesn't beat me!" Touching her face she whispers, "He's just got a rough touch."

"He blackens your eyes!" I emphasize during the process of clearing away the condom wrappers, cigarette butts, and wiping the surfaces down to be livable.

"It's nothing make-up can't cover!" My mother returns to screaming probably scaring my daughter like usual.

"He's a waste of great God given space and shouldn't be around my mother let alone my Goddamn daughter!" I fling the fallen pillows onto the couch.

"You're so selfish! Everything's always about you!"

"About me?" I whisper. Turning around, I raise my voice, "About me? Worrying about you and my daughter is being selfish? I protect you day in and day out through your drunken episodes, and this is the thanks I get?"

"I don't need your protection."

"Clearly. What was he doing here anyway? Didn't I give you money already?"

With a sneer she rolls her eyes, "I've got bills to pay and needed more money than I had."

"Bills to pay or alcohol to drink?"

"Bills, Connor."

"And you couldn't ask me for the money?"

"Ugh, don't give me that." She flicks her wrist at me. "You know you have to support MaKayla. Besides, I'm a grown woman. I can take care of myself."

"Obviously."

"You shouldn't talk to me like that. I am your mother, you know," she sighs, her buzz beginning to wear off.

"Only biologically," I respond, relocating our backpacks to the living room.

Ignoring my comment she continues, "And he *is* your stepfather."

My movement stops. "Only lawfully. He will never be any sort of father to me. Ever."

"Why not? It's not like your dad is coming back from the grave!"

"And if he did the first fucking thing he would do is congratulate me for not letting that garbage stay in this house!"

"You need to show me some respect," the request seems more than mildly dumb.

Turning to look at her, I state coldly, "Earn it."

For a moment she merely looks at me, swollen eyes a bit watery, bruised jaw slightly trembling, and possibly broken hand shaking as it tries to find a place to rest on her fragile frame. With a deep breath to either ease the physical pain her early 40s body continuously encounters, or the emotional pain of having to live with being a terrible mother, with a son who possibly doesn't love her, she simply sighs, "I'm going to lie down. I'll see you in the morning."

I move my glance to the remaining trash for me to pick up at the same time her door slams shut. Annoyed, I flop down on the couch and bury my face in my hands. As my fingertips massage my head, I listen to the muffled sound of my mother's tears. Life wasn't always like this. There wasn't always this battle zone with a line drawn in the sand. She once loved me like a mother should love a son. Took care of me. Of her. Of my dad...I guess that's the worst part of watching someone you love die and taking care of them in the process. You lose a part of yourself you can never grow back. I know this. Just like I know that I need to do the right thing. Be the man my father expected me to be when he died. With a long exhale, I stand up and retreat to her room seeing her sprawled out with tears stained on her face.

Sliding next to her, I grab the purple blanket and cover her with it. Her tears continue to fall before I hear her whimper, "I try so hard to...to...to..."

"I know Mom," My hand caresses her back trying to calm her down. "I know."

"And I get it Connor. I'm not very good at this whole mother thing anymore."

"You're not too terrible when you're actually trying."

"Right. And how often is that?"

I bite my tongue as best as I can, "You know one way to get better is to 86 this whole drugs thing. You're killing yourself not to mention making it really hard to raise a kid here. If you're not going to fix things for yourself or me, at least do it for Mak. She needs her grandmother in her life and at this rate…you won't be."

Her head bobs like it does every time we have this conversation. Even though I know all I've done is waste my breath, I have to keep trying. Faith. Belief. Never giving up. Basic life principles Dad would say. Even dead, with so much of his memory faded from me, he still stands the most reliable guide in this shit storm I call my life. I tuck my mother in and kiss her forehead.

"I'll let Mak sneak in here once you've sobered up a bit to tell you goodnight."

"Thanks Connor." She touches her swelling eye.

"Want some ice for that?"

Immediately she shakes her head and rolls over, the faint sound of tears starting up again.

Leaving her room I close the door shut and head to the bathroom where I admire the amazing bruise developing on my face. I run my thumb across the discoloring, not surprised so much as annoyed that I have to create another excuse for coming to school with faded marks that appear to be that of abuse. Doesn't matter now like it did before I was 18. Most of my classmates think I'm in some sort of underground fighting circle. Brent had something to do with that after a girl he was dating was obsessed with a book about an MMA fighter. Said it would make a great cover story. Surprisingly enough he never asked what was actually causing the bruises.

After wrapping some ice in a towel and pressing it against my jaw, I release Mak from our bedroom. Still clutching her teddy bear, she slinks out, and directly into my arms. Mac's head rests on my shoulder as she sniffles frightened, something she is a little too often for me to feel like a successful parent.

"You okay Princess?"

After receiving a nod she points to where I'm holding the ice, "Boo-boo?"

"I'll be okay."

"I don't like when you get ouchies Daddy."

"Me either," I mumble and adjust her in my grip. "How about I heat you up some pizza and turn on a movie?"

"Cinderella?" Her head pops up.

"Didn't we just watch that a couple days ago?"

Mak whines, "Cinderella daddy. I wanna watch Cinderella."

"I know Princess but—"

"Please," her green eyes threaten to fill with tears. "Please. Pretty please."

"Alright," I give in sitting her down on the couch. "Grab the DVD."

While Mak rummages around searching for the movie, I heat up pizza for us, grab fruit and drinks as well as my script. Once we're both settled, I focus more on reviewing my lines, rehearsing them quietly to myself as my little girl sings along to the movie.

Mak taps me on the shoulder at the same part she always does. "Look Daddy! They said Cinderella could go to the ball!"

"I know," my voice hums as I shove a pepperoni in my mouth. "Princess, why do you love this movie so much?"

"'Cause..." She reaches for an apple slice.

"Because what?"

"Because Cinderella gets Prince Charming and they get to be together like a Mommy and a Daddy should be!"

Feeling a sudden ache, like my heart is being burned alive, I question in a weary voice, "Is that...is that what you hope for when you watch this? Do you hope for a Mommy and Daddy?"

"I do! I do! I get a mommy too! I believe it!"

Muscling through the pain I nod my head not comfortable with killing her hope. Someone in this house has to have enough to keep the rest of us going. I just wish...I just wish she could have normal hopes for her age. Like for a pony. Or to actually *be* a princess.

"We not there yet."

"Not where?"

"At happily ever after."

"Happily ever after?"

"Yes. I don't know when. It's soon," Mak smiles widely at me. "It has to be Daddy! It just has to be..."

The combination of the words, the tone, and the sheer faith in them are enough to force me to toss my script to the side. I watch as my daughter lives in her own dream world, a world free from poverty and troubles, a world free from struggle and shame, a world where money isn't important or if it is, it's not nearly as important as love. A world where she has a mommy and a daddy. A world I dream of providing her day in and day out.

"Can I have your 'ronis Daddy?" Mak wiggles her fingers at my pizza.

"Of course Princess." I push my plate at her. In a soft whisper I say, "Daddy will give you anything he can. I promise." She grabs a hand full of cheese off the pizza capturing one of the pepperonis. I do my best to force a smile on my face knowing my appetite for food has been replaced with my hunger for the only escape I get from the pathetic reality of my life. Sleep.

Chapter 5

The following Tuesday in theater Ms. Flores begins the minute the bell rings, something out of the norm for her. "Today we're going to do an exercise with your characters. I want you and your partner to pair up and discuss the real life similarities you have with them and what real life similarities you think your partner has with theirs. I'll be coming around to see what progress has been made around towards the end of class."

Great. Another get to know you exercise. Heaven knows we don't do enough of those or anything. Ms. Flores dismisses us, allowing us to find comfortable spaces to pair up. To no surprise, we end up in the back corner aka Gianna's lair.

Yanking out her script she grumbles, "This seems like a dumb exercise."

"I don't think so. Part of acting is getting to know which part of you relates to what you're portraying."

"Why do you always agree with everything Ms. Flores says?"

"Because she's usually right."

"Your cock usually points up for her so that means she's right?"

I grip my script tighter. "Do you have some sort of goal to try to piss me off in the first five minutes you're around me?"

Innocently smirking, she leans back, black sweater dress inching up her firm toned thighs. "That's one way of putting it."

"Well let's see if you keep that goal when I leave class to go tell Principle Smith that this arrangement isn't really working out."

"Now why do you always have to take it there?" She sighs sitting up straight. "Can't you ever just defend yourself?"

"I have no problem defending myself. It's just a wasted effort to fight with someone who I could just as easily remove from my life." I have enough problems making my life difficult without adding to them.

"That's your problem right there. Just like your character. You always want to take the easy way out. Sure, it's easier to get me kicked out of school and you a brand new partner, just like it's easy for your character to break up with mine than actually fight for her."

My jaw slips down, baffled for a moment, "You...you...you…you've actually read your script? *And* given it thought?"

Gianna starts to gather her hair up into a pony tail. "Eh, a tad."

Impressed, but not willing to admit it, I simply lean forward and rest my arms on my legs. "So what do you have in common with your character?"

"We're both beautiful."

A smile paints itself on my face before I shake my head. "While yes that's true--"

"It is?" She grins wildly. "You think I'm beautiful."

Softly I say, "I'd have to be blind not to and even then I'm sure I'd know it." Realizing I let a compliment slip, I try to push past it, "How about we try for something a little less superficial?"

"Like what? We both love green, like your eyes?"

Her simple attempt to return the gesture doesn't escape me, but I don't give into it, "I said less superficial, not more."

"Maybe that isn't superficial. Green is a color that can represent power and wealth, something we both find necessary to have even though in her case she loses more and more as the play progresses."

Dumbfounded she's already given this that much thought, I say, "I guess that would be less superficial."

"Thank you."

"You might want to be careful with which color you choose to tie to your character with. For instance, green can also represent an enormous amount of greed and selfishness."

Her eyebrows raise and she leans forward to whisper, "I know you think I'm selfish and if you've read the script like I have you know she's selfish too, so it seems to me that green is the best color to be our favorite."

My lips press together as I nod. The girl is two for two in less than 5 minutes. Warm up before the real game?

"As the second part of this exercise, you're supposed to tell me what you think we have in common. So come on, you tell me what you think I have in common with her. You know, other than you think we're beautiful."

My head tilts to the side as I study Gianna today in her tight dress where I can see the way her body curves, the perfect shape of her tits, and the unbelievable smoothness to the heavy artillery she calls legs. Unconsciously, my tongue slides out of my mouth at the thought of my hands touching them.

"And now besides my measurements," her hand lifts my face back up. "What do we have in common?"

"I think you're both hiding something." Gianna suddenly looks slightly uncomfortable. "I mean, Catherine is hiding the affair from her husband, but there's a reasons she's having an affair to begin with right? Because there's a part of her that she's not being true to. There's something there she doesn't want the audience to know, something there she doesn't want her husband to know, something there that the only person who can understand it is essentially my character. He's the only person she trusts because he's having an affair for the same reason. There's something they both feel they can't share with their partners. They've got secrets and only trust each other."

"So..." She leans down so her face is closer to mine. "Do you trust me?"

"No," I bluntly respond, which clearly upsets her. With a small grin I whisper, "But I'd like to change that. Would you?"

Her jaw slides open to answer my question, when the fire alarm ironically enough goes off. Sign from above? Should we call that warning bells? Hell...yeah...those have to be warning bells. I can't get close to this girl. I just can't.

"Alright students walk calmly," Ms. Flores yells over the screeching sound of the alarm. All thirty six of us scramble out of the classroom, down the hall, and out the back entrance to the cafeteria. Once outside we follow with the rest of the crowd across the faculty parking lot, heading to the area by the field house.

"Connor," Brent calls to me leaving his gym class mob to meet up with me. "Sup."

I toss him a head nod as a return greeting.

"You think something is actually on fire?" his question seems dumb, but then again, they usually announce planned fire drills not to instill mass fear and chaos. Last time we had an unannounced drill the cafeteria smelled of burnt tater tots for what felt like months.

"Maybe," I sigh and glance over my shoulder just in time to notice Gianna who's swaying back and forth alone. Even looking lonely like that she's still something that my eyes can't help but wander over to. Friends. We can be friends. Everyone needs a friend. Even if it's a distant friend, everyone needs at least one. "Hey, Brent, I think you might've met her the other day but in case you forgot, this is Gianna. She's my theater partner."

"Yeah." Brent smiles and extends his hand. "Gianna, I'm Brent."

Surprised, she stops twirling her pony tail to shake back. "Nice to meet you."

"So you guys were in theater?" He asks, his eyes wandering behind me at Nicole Simon, the only girl I've ever seen him remotely interested in. Between the fact I've sworn off chicks and all of Brent's attention is on Nicole, Bret swears every chance he gets we're the worst wing men a guy could have outside of video games.

"Yeah, practice makes perfect."

Brent's eyes don't wander back even as he asks, "Wanna ball when you get out or you still gotta work today?"

"Work. Sorry man."

"It's cool." He shrugs attention finally peeled away from Nicole. "I'll catch you later then. Coach is starting to take count."

I give him a nod before he hustles away. Looking back at Gianna who's doing her best to hide a grin. The two of us stand side by side in silence, not uttering another word. First flirting, now introducing her to my friends. Not gonna end well if I don't cut this shit out. And fast.

Chapter 6

At lunch the next day, I'm eating alone, much like I always do on Wednesday, when Gianna plops herself in front of me with a diet soda and a smile. A beautiful, kind smile. One that's a little different than I've seen on her in the past. I kind of like it. Ugh. I can't like it. I look around briefly confused if she meant to sit in front of me, I just watch, waiting for her to say something.

When she doesn't seem to say anything, I put my fork down and ask, "Can I help you?"

"No, just thought maybe you didn't wanna eat alone."

I shrug. "It's kind of a normal thing on Wednesdays."

"Why?"

"Bret and Brent usually go play ball on the outside court during lunch time."

"And you don't like basketball?"

"I do."

"Then why don't you play? Are you not good at it? Is basketball not fun for you?"

"It is. I love it actually."

"Then I repeat, why don't you play?"

"Occasionally I do." Like on the days I don't have enough lunch money to feed myself. "Most of the time, this is the only chance I get to eat before work."

"That makes sense." Gianna takes a sip of her soda, my eyes darting down to her lips. "But you don't think you could just stomach through the day and go all out for dinner?"

"By the time I get off and end up making dinner--"

"Wait, you make dinner? Like you can cook?"

Mak's face pops into my mind. "I have no choice but to cook."

"Mom and Dad can't?"

The question has me adjusting on the bench and reaching for a chip. Both of my parents were great cooks. When Mom started spending more time at the hospital than at home, I started to learn. "I really don't mind eating alone Gianna."

Ignoring my comment she says, "I have an answer to your question from yesterday."

I prepare to play stupid when she raises her eyebrows as if daring me too. Of course I didn't forget the question. It was the first time I openly offered friendship to someone of the opposite sex in years. I replayed the damn situation in my head like a song stuck on repeat, trying to figure out what the hell happened. How the hell did I slip? Are the hardships I wake up to everyday not serving as a good enough reminder anymore?

"You mean about changing the trust thing between us?"

"Yeah..." She fiddles with her soda bottle and nibbles on her bottom lip.

"Okay." I wipe my hands and my mouth, trying to keep my attention on her eyes and not her tight pink sweater that looks like it's two sizes too small on her chest. I wonder how she looks out of that sweater. "You don't wanna wait 'til we get to class to talk about it?"

"No," her answer is followed by a strand of hair falling into her face bringing my attention to how much more beautiful she is when she wears less make up. Why is she wearing less make up? "I wanted to talk about it before, which is why I approached you at lunch."

"I thought it was because you didn't want me eating alone?" I tease.

She snickers a bit and shakes her head with a similar playful attitude, "Ugh. That too. Whatever."

Balling up my fist I rest my chin on it. "Alright, you have my attention. I'm all ears. So what's your answer?"

"I do." The response is exactly what I wanted, but definitely not what I needed.

"Good deal." I smile and pick my fork back up to finish my salad. Moments from taking another bite, I can't help but notice the look of how anxious she is about something. Her fingers toy with hair and she starts nibbling on her bottom lip again. Placing it back down I lean forward, "Is there something on your mind in particular you wanna talk to me about?"

With a short shoulder shrug she says, "Kind of..."

"Go ahead."

"Well," she hums out looking around the busy cafeteria. "Um..."

Looking at my pretty much finished lunch, I ask, "Wanna go back by the performance building and talk?"

"That sounds good."

With one more bite of my sandwich and one more bite of a chip, I throw my trash away and start towards the back exit of the cafeteria with Gianna at my side, catching the attention of a few known gossip starters. Might as well let them talk about something other than my fictional boxing career.

After a trip to the bathroom that takes what feels like five minutes, she rushes out, freshens her breath, and the two of us start walking outside, side by side, just waiting for someone to say something.

"So…" I slip my hands in my dark denim pockets.

"I wouldn't say I'm hiding so much as running from past mistakes," she adjusts her shoulder bag.

"You're running?"

"More like sprinting. Like who needs to run a marathon when this bitch can run in stilettos."

Stopping at the outside of the building I lean my back against it. "At least you look good in stilettos."

"Thanks."

"Question is, what has you running to begin with?"

Gianna suddenly lets her eyes wander off in the distance for a moment before she directs her attention at me. "I've been kicked out of nine schools in a year and half. Four private, two public, and three religious related schools. We've left Paris, New York, L.A. and Atlanta because of me."

"Why were you kicked out?"

"You name it. I did it." She moves her body to lean against the building beside me.

Seeing she's not going to be specific without help I decide to be straightforward, "Drugs?"

"Did 'em."

"Which ones?"

"From the well-known ones? It would just be easier to ask me which ones I didn't do," she uncomfortably chuckles.

"Okay. What haven't you done?"

"Crack, because that seems lame and heroine because well, inserting needles into my skin doesn't roll over too well with me."

"You have a tat."

"You saw that?" She wiggles her eyebrows at me.

It's hard to miss the infinity symbol of stars on the back of her thigh. It gives an entirely different meaning to aiming for the stars.

"You're picturing it now," she teases, elbowing me jokingly in the ribs.

"I...I..wasn't," my lie is followed with a huge smile I can't fight. Something about when this girl smiles makes the urge to smile infectious. Turning my face to see her smiling brightly I roll my eyes, "Oh shut up. You know it's sexy."

"Yeah, but a little appreciation never hurts a girl's feelings." Gianna winks.

The possibility of this conversation turning the direction that could make my jeans tighter forces me to insist on refocusing on the topic. Otherwise I'm gonna end up doing something I regret more than I did offering her a friendship, which now seems like something she needed more than I would have ever imagined. "My point was they do tattoos with a needle."

"Yeah, but that's different. That's like a doodle on your flesh. It wasn't shoved in my veins and…" She shutters at the thought. "Whatever. I've smoked pot in the back of one of my parent's voting parties. I've done coke at their socialite fundraisers. Ecstasy with friends at parties and school events. Mushrooms on bus rides. Should I continue?"

"No that's a pretty clear picture. Why though? What's the point?"

Innocently she shrugs. "Fun, duh."

"Of course. I've always imagined putting things in my body that could essentially kill me or build an unhealthy addiction to as fun. It's seemed to be as much fun as having someone rip off my nuts and then ask me to reattach them myself."

"Graphic."

"I try."

"Anyway, it was fun or at least it felt that way. I mean come on....I started doing shit before puberty that most people don't even think about until they're in their 20s. I mean what choice did I have?"

Turning so my shoulder is leaning against the wall I ask, "What do you mean?"

Gianna takes a deep breath, bracing herself to answer, "I used to be a model."

"Really?"

"Really. Really. My father knows the who's who of the business, and so if I had a dream, it came true. I modeled for a few years, just mainstream basics, suggestive tops, jeans, swimsuits, but I got caught up in trying to stay thin and fit in. Basically fell into the whole model cliché, which isn't what my parents wanted, so they cut me off. They took me out of the world I loved, the world I had grown to understand, the world that had basically become me, and threw me into teen...hood...or whatever the hell this nightmare is."

I fucking know that feeling better than anyone else. Being stuck growing up faster than you can handle. Ditching basketballs games for trips to the ER with your dying parent. Skipping prom to change diapers. Lying about the vacation you took during Spring Break because you're ashamed your lights were cut off for most of the week. Yeah. It's safe to say I understand this girl on a whole other level. Part of me is thankful for that. It'll make it easier for her to get me someday. Wait. What am I saying? That's not gonna happen.

"I know that's not easy."

"Are you kidding? It was a breeze," her sarcasm makes me smirk as she smirks at me. "When it all came crashing down, we were still living primarily in New York, so I stayed in the same amount of trouble. My friends and I all had mommy and daddy's money to cover up the mistakes, so why care? Why stop running my life into the ground if they're just going to bail me out, you know?"

My head shakes side to side, "No. Not at all." Her body turns to mimic mine. "I don't know at all what that's like. There's no one to take care of my mistakes, but me, and that's dumb if that's your excuse for doing stupid shit. I mean did you even enjoy any of it?"

"Occasionally."

"Occasionally? You mean to tell me you literally just did it to do it? That's fucking stupid."

"What's fucking stupid is the fact I couldn't realize that faster, before I was relocated every thirty seconds because I couldn't stop! I had to go to rehab in order to stop!" Suddenly I feel like a dick. Uncomfortable with how quick I was to jump down her throat I scratch the back of my neck. I know better than to judge anyone else like that. Look at my life. "I was in and out of rehab for almost eight months! Moving here is the last resort. When I finally finished a program, they moved me here, to this weird ass, soul sucking, suicide place known as suburbia, and told me if I so much as looked at another drug they'd ship me off. My father has pulled every string in the book to keep his name clean by keeping my name clean and it has cost him a fortune, not to mention his hair. One wrong move and I'm gone. So I don't have any friends. No friends means no temptation. No friends means no one can judge me for the shit I've done. I'm running from my past. I don't ever try to face it and blame myself for what happened. In my house we never talk about what happened. Everyone pretends it never did, so I'm running. Sprinting. Sprinting from the reality of the fact I've destroyed my life and don't know how to pick up the pieces."

Knowing that exact feeling has me wanting to do something that I know I shouldn't. But that's the story of my entire life now. Avoiding things I shouldn't. Not wanting anything because it's not right. Because Mak should be the only thing I focus on. And she is. She always will be. I'd rather die than let Mak not feel like she matters to me, but does that mean I can't, even for a moment, just have something for me? Can't having a friend, one who has no one else, be an okay thing?

I push past the nagging feeling that this is the wrong decision and wrap my arms around Gianna tightly. Her arms fling around me as her head hits my chest, soft sobs vibrating her chest against mine.

"There." She sniffles louder. "There's my sob story." How is it that what lies underneath that bitchy exterior is sexier and sweeter than what I was imaging? "But don't tell okay?"

"I won't," I sigh as she squeezes me tighter. Lost in the sensation of having a girl in my arms, I let my eyes drift closed. God, it's been so long since...well since I've even let myself touch someone like this. I know you can't get someone pregnant from hugging them, but still. My fingers softly stroke her back thankful that even if this is the only contact I get to have with the opposite sex for another couple years, that at least I got it. And at least it's with her. "It's our secret Gianna."

Chapter 7

Over the next couple of weeks in theater, Gianna and I grow closer and closer, which isn't the best idea I know, but I can't seem to help it. There's just something about her. Sometimes it's the things she says that I think no one else ever felt but me. Sometimes it's the way we laugh together like it's just us in the world. Sometimes it's just the way we argue until we're damn near ready to kill each other. Those are the times that worry me. Most of them end with us fuming and a little something unexplainable will happen to break the tension. To force us back to neutral ground. It feels like some outside force trying to keep us on the same path. Dad would say that's what happens when you have faith in life. It'll take you exactly where you really wanna go. Problem is, other than being a great dad to Mak, I'm not sure where that is. An actor would be an amazing path but there's not enough stability there in the long run....but who knows? Maybe something in that field. Maybe not. I gotta graduate first. That's one path I know for sure.

As we take the stage, laughing about something that happened to her in English, she drops her bag and smiles proudly. "You know, I know all my lines now. Script free."

"Really?" I ask, excited that maybe we'll actually make more progress. "That's awesome."

"Proud?"

"Definitely."

She giggles while the sound of her brown leather knee high boots echos in the auditorium as she crosses the stage. "I'm ready now. I'm ready to start working scene by scene. So, director..." Gianna bites her bottom lip, hands seductively falling to her hips, "Whatever you want, wherever you want is fine by me."

The invitation for something my dick hasn't had in years has me needing a moment to gain my composure. Tempting doesn't even start to describe the level my feelings are on. I've been so caught up in reveries of her that it's taking longer to do my homework at night not to mention how many nights I've lost sleep over fantasizing about what I wanna do to her and with her. Nothing better to will away the urge to whack it like your two year old landing her tiny balled up fist in your ribs.

I shed my leather jacket and adjust my t-shirt noticing the long intense stare she has with every movement I make. No. No. Friends. We can only be friends. And even that is stretching my limits beyond points of comfort.

Clearing my throat in hopes of regaining our focus, I approach her, "Let's take it from the scene where you're trying to tell me our affair is over."

"Really? This is a sad part, you know."

"I know. I've read it."

"And you couldn't have started with a happy moment? I mean we were just laughing like 2 minutes ago."

"I want to see you stretch."

"I can bend over."

Lightly chuckling I shake my head, "You can and while the view is one that doesn't disappoint, I mean with your emotions. I wanna see you happy when you're sad and sad when you're happy. It's important to have a steady handle on your emotions. As much as you want your emotions to drive your character and your performance, it's important to have a good grip on them. Filming on screen doesn't get filmed in any particular order, so it's great skill to perfect, the sooner the better."

"How do you know I wanna act on screen?"

"Call it a hunch," Gianna folds her arms across her chest disapprovingly. "Fine," my hands toss in the air, "because you don't seem like the snootiness of the theater is your pace. Besides with your past history of being a model, the Hollywood choice would be the most likely route. Am I wrong?"

She gives a short shoulder shrug like I struck an unwanted nerve. "Can we just start?"

I position myself a few feet behind her, take a deep breath, and slide into character.

"Nick," she sighs and looks down at her feet. "This…this relationship, this…affair, this thing, this thing between us is over."

"Why Catherine?" I rush towards her concern painted on my face. "Why?"

"I love my husband." Gianna looks up at me, the lie clear.

"You do not."

"I do." Her tone lifts, like she almost believes it. "This affair was just poor timing." She starts fidgeting and it seems overacted. I make a mental note to come back to it. "This was just one giant mistake. This was all just—"

"Perfect," my voice whimpers as my arms fly around her waist, cradling her body closer to mine. "This has been so perfect. I've never felt the way I feel about you with any other woman, including my own wife. I want to be with you. I want us to be together."

She slightly pushes me as she takes a step back, "No."

Grabbing her arm, I spin her around and wrap her even closer to me, "Stay." My fingertips stroke her hips while staring into her eyes. With a tone dripped in pleading I beg, "Be with me." Her eyes lift with hope. "What can he do for you that I can't?"

"He--"

"Does he love you like I do? Can he hold you the way I do? Can he stare into your eyes," my eyes fall deeper into hers before I push the hair out of her face, "and tell you that you're the only person in the entire world for him?"

"No..." she whispers melting into my arms. "He doesn't."

"Because he can't."

"That's not the point," Gianna says her voice sounding nothing like her own. "I love him."

My forehead presses against hers. "Like I love you baby?"

Her breathing suddenly changes and she grips the edge of my shirt, a well planted action on her part. I make note of that too. "No one can love me like you do."

"Then don't leave. Stay. Run away with me," I beg. "Please Catherine."

"I..." Gianna stumbles over her lines. "I...I...I..."

Doing my best to help her move along I whisper, "You?"

"I wanna kiss you," she whimpers.

Confused I croak, "What?"

"I wanna kiss you."

Nervous, I reply, "That's um not in the script."

"I know." And without giving me another chance to object Gianna's soft, sticky lips land on mine, the sweetest of sighs falling out of her at the same time. Wanting to fight back, knowing I can't kiss back, that I can't take this a step further, my mouth goes to pull back when her tongue snakes out tasting my bottom lip. At that moment, all will power flies out the window. My mouth parts

63

desperate to have just a sample of what has had my mind going in circles. Soft and slow is my intention, but the fact this is the only girl I've kissed since Mak was born has my body behaving everything but gentle. I grip her a little tighter and push my tongue harder against hers, pleased when she makes that sweet sigh once more.

"Connor and Gianna," Ms. Flores' voice cuts through our kiss.

Immediately we fly apart, her with a gorgeous guilty grin, and me wiping away my mouth in anxiousness.

Ms. Flores approaches us. "I'm sorry I haven't been able to give you a small review yet, but, I figured you could handle yourself Connor," she compliments. "I mean you always have. Anyway here I am to see whatever it is you've been working on."

"Can I go to the bathroom first?" Gianna asks, running her fingers through her hair.

I raise my eyebrows at Gianna who seems to go to the bathroom the same time every day even though I tell her to go before we get into class. At first I swore she did it to annoy me, then for makeup refresher, but I've seen her reapply her lip gloss too often during class for that to be the reason.

Doing my best to distract myself I ask, "How are Nicole and Jake doing?"

"Pretty good. Coming along rather well, but I hope you two are progressing even better. You know how much I hope you get this Connor," she answers glancing around me, "for obvious and unobvious reasons."

"You and me both."

About five minutes later, Gianna returns, freshens her breath with a mint strip, and takes the stage to show Ms. Flores she can dedicate herself when she chooses to.

Chapter 8

The rest of the week the two of us engage in several kissing sessions around the school. One in the library behind the dusty non-fiction books, two in the cafeteria close to the bathrooms no one uses most of the time, three outside on our walk to theater, and of course goodbye kisses in the parking lot before parting. At first the kisses started with a tense nagging sensation that I shouldn't be kissing her at all, but it began to vanish faster and faster until I got to the point it didn't come at all. In fact the opposite did. Excitement. Longing. Wondering how long until I'll get just one more moment to kiss. Kissing Gianna is quickly fading from a mistake that happened during rehearsal and growing into a sexy sin that feels like heaven. The major problem is I'm still paying for the last sexy sin I engaged in. I can't let myself forget that.

On Friday, our theater teacher is absent and wants us to take our class time to continue working as we have been in our pairs. Luckily, our substitute agrees to let me and Gianna go to the library to 'research' background information on our characters for the remainder of the class period.

Strolling, our hands locked together, Gianna giggles, "You wanna skip and just go to my house?"

Immediately I shake my head, "Nah. Not into that."

"Have you *ever* skipped school before?"

"Once or twice."

"Wow. That's it? You need to live a little."

"Thanks," I sarcastically reply.

"Sorry." Gianna nibbles on her bottom lip before stopping in the middle of the empty courtyard. Her arms slide up around my neck as she pleads, "Come on Connor. Just this once. Skip with me and I'll never ask you to do it again."

Mockingly I shoot her a look.

"Okay, I'll probably ask you to do it again," the confession has us both slightly laughing. My hands wrap around her tighter. There's something about having her in my arms that I can't get enough of. It's dangerous to get this attached, but damn, it feels good. "But not any time soon. Please..."

"I can't Baby. I have to be at work in less than a couple of hours."

"I know, but I don't live that far."

"Really?"

"Really. I promise, you won't be late for work."

Still hesitant I question, "Really?"

"Really. You trust me right?" The question is one that I can't stomach answering truthfully. I do. I trust her in ways I haven't trusted anyone since my father died. I trust with my heart that I didn't even know beat for anyone other than Mak. But then there's Mak. I haven't told her. I don't know that I should. Hell, I don't know if I can. I don't know if I trust anyone else knowing anything about that bright green eyed princess of mine. "Connor, you do trust me right?"

Instead of answering the question I lean down and place a brief kiss on her lips. "Am I following you in my car?"

Gianna lets it go as soon as she realizes she's getting her way. "I'll drive!"

"They let you have a license?"

With a playful slap on the chest she giggles, "Shut up."

I smile and let her lead me towards the parking lot where she sneaks us off campus by lying to the parking attendant with fake tears and a sob story about a sick pet, proving without a doubt the girl really can act. In Gianna's black 2015 Benz, we pull out of the parking lot. Settling into the leather I try to swallow the lump of envy that's grown in my throat. It's not her fault she was born to rich parents any more than it's my fault my father's death left us with next to nothing. I glance over as she slides on her designer sunglasses looking like something out of a celebrity gossip mag. What in the hell am I doing?

At the stop light a couple minutes down the road from the school, Gianna leans over, puts a hand on my cheek, and turns my face to let our lips meet again. Our tongues briefly touch before she pulls away, leaving the obvious answer to my question. I'm falling for a girl. Slowly, but fucking surely.

About five minutes down the road that runs parallel to the side of the school, we take a turn onto a windy road, with houses few and far between to find a giant, gated off mansion, with a security guard waiting for people to arrive. The princess really does live in a palace. No wonder she acts like the world is at her beck and call. It really is.

"Good afternoon Ms. Gianna," the guard sighs leaning through his open window. The sunlight reflects off of his bald white head and his badge. While he doesn't seem too intimidating to me, I can imagine the gun on his hip probably helps. "What are you doing off early?"

Pushing her sunglasses into her hair she innocently smiles. "Free period. Claimed I was going to the library, decided to come home and study my lines with my partner instead."

"So you're skipping school again?" His chubby fingers tap the desk.

"That's the negative way to look at it."

"That's the accurate way to look at it."

"That's what I said."

"Gianna," he scolds. "You know you shouldn't be skipping school especially not with a guy."

"Well mom," she sarcastically starts, "I may not be in school, but I'm still studying. More importantly he's not just any guy. He's...well he's my partner for my acting class."

"Is this acting class partner thing code for sex tape companion?"

"Whoa," I surrender my hands in the air to the guard. "No. No. No. No...."

"Acting like theater. As in my class for school."

"Mmhm," the guard leans back in his chair. "Which should be done *at* school."

"Are you going to open the gate or not?" Gianna snaps.

"Not."

"Do you want those chocolate chip cookies tonight or should I just give them to Sally?"

Fidgeting with things around the button, he ends up hitting it to open the gate, "Have a good afternoon."

Smiling victoriously she smirks. "We will. Are Mom and Dad home?"

"Your mother is getting her hair and nails done followed by a late massage. Your father is having a lunch meeting downtown and then cocktails with that director at The Q. House is parental unit free for most of the evening."

67

"Thank you," she says almost a hint of sadness to her voice. No, I don't like when my mother's home and high or wasted but at least she comes home. At least there are times when she's sober and we eat together. From the way the guard outlined their schedules I get the sneaking suspicion Gianna doesn't see them often or maybe as often as she wants. I could be wrong though.

Driving through the gate and onto the property I gawk at the open yard that has exotic birds grazing on it, trees trimmed like buildings from different cities, and statues the height of some trees. Everything is abundantly green and lush, which is impressive considering it is winter.

I admire the Olympic size pool in the front yard area that you can get to by following a beautiful stone path. "Nice pool."

"Yeah. It's okay since it's just the front pool."

"You've got two pools?"

"We've got three," her answer is nonchalant as she pulls around into the circle drive way in front of the house. "I'll just park here for now."

Baffled I stutter, "You-You-You've got three pools?"

"The small one you saw, the infinity in the back, and the heated one on the third floor in the gym."

My jaw bobs in amazement, unsure of what to say.

Gianna kills the engine and winks. "We can try out all three instead of doing lines if you want."

The sexual suggestion kicks my brain into working and I shake my head. "Lines. We're gonna run lines."

"Can we make out a little?" She tries to look innocent.

Unable to resist her I plant a quick peck on her lips. "Let's get going. Clock's ticking."

The two of us get out and enter the largest place I've ever seen a human being live in real life. Back when I had time to watch trashy television and there was nothing else on, I remember seeing homes like this from the different celebrities with reality shows. I remember being in awe that any family, forget about any one person, needing that much space or that much shit. That those people just spent money to spend money. I promised myself at that point, while my father lay wasting away that I would never do that. If I ever made money like that, there's no way in hell I'd piss it away on useless shit.

Gianna doesn't bother with giving me a tour. Her mind is on one thing and one thing only. If I didn't have Mak to constantly remind me why that's a terrible idea, my head would be right there with hers. She leads me by the hand from the door directly up the set of grand stairs you are greeted with when you walk in. At the point where they split, she takes the right side to the top, takes another right and heads to the very end of the hallway.

My eyes widen at the room that's the same size as my entire apartment.

Immediately she walks over to her California king sized bed that's off to the side in its own nook. Gianna flops down on top of her stuffed animals while she kicks off her heels. Continuing to admire the unbelievable sight, I look around seeing an office like area where there's a built into the wall desk with a hutch, a desk top computer, two lap tops, an Ipad plugged in next to some sort of other tablet. There are four book shelves overflowing with books, two on each side of the desk.

Tilting my head towards the books I ask, "You like to read?"

"Sometimes," she hums.

Not too far from that area there's a mini fridge, a standing storage cabinet that looks like it might contain snacks, and a microwave. My eyes keep moving around the room taking notice of an entertainment area where she has a flat screen mounted on the wall, rows and rows of Blue-rays on built into the wall shelves. On a glass table underneath the TV there's a cable box, the latest XBOX, Play Station, and Wii. The two recliners are positioned to where she can still see the TV from her bed if she wants. If all that wasn't possibly enough I notice next to her door that probably leads to her bathroom that I am assuming is as huge as her room, is another door cracked open that I assume is her walk in closet.

"You like my room?" the question causes the corner of my mouth to tilt up while I beat down the envy that's steadily growing.

"That's one way of putting it," I mumble heading for one of the black recliners. On my way to the chair I notice the typical chick posters of Marilyn Monroe are mixed in with various framed posters of her. She looks younger in the photos, but just as attention grabbing as ever. Some of the photos have her in suggestive clothing, others in swim wear, but all accenting the one thing I noticed about her from day one, those Goddamn legs. "Damn you were a good looking model."

Gianna slightly scoffs, "Were?"

Smiling at her I shake my head, "Chill out. You're still beautiful. You know that."

"Ya know," she struts' seductively over me, my eyes dropping down to her thighs that my hands are itching to run themselves up. "You're hard to resist when you call me beautiful."

Gianna straddles my lap and I wrap my hands on her hips. "Is that right?"

She bites her bottom lip playfully before leaning down to kiss me. For just a moment I forget that we came to rehearse, that it's a bad idea to be making out with her all the time, and the consequences of being so careless. My hands slide around, giving her ass the simple squeeze they've been dying too. As soon as Gianna moans and grinds herself against me, I know I have to stop. We can't go there. We just...can't.

Pulling back, I sigh, "Lines. We agreed to run lines."

"Fine. Fine." She replies sliding off my lap. "You want a snack first? You didn't eat lunch." While part of the reason I didn't eat lunch was because I was too busy making out with her, the other is the fact, I'm drained for extra money already. "I've got tons of shit. Basically anything you want you can have and if I don't have it up here, I can tell Betty to make something you want."

The idea that she has that kind of power and isn't grateful for it, has me threatening to say something I shouldn't. Instead I push that down and shrug, "I'll take a soda or some chips or something."

Gianna prances off, grabbing snacks for us, rehearsal of just line by line beginning during the process. It's good measure to know all lines and being able to start them at the drop of dime no matter the part of the scene you start at. We go round and round for a while munching. Midway discussing some new blocking ideas, Gianna excuses herself to the restroom.

While I wait for her to return, my eyes start accessing the room again, admiring particularly her photos that I know if they were hanging in my bedroom exactly what I would do with them. Suddenly I hear a sound that forces me to walk over to the bathroom door and press my ear up against it hearing the sound in a louder volume. Between having an alcoholic for a mother and a small child who has had her fair share of upset stomachs, I know exactly what that sound is. In a panic, I barge in seeing Gianna leaned over the toilet, her hair pulled back in her hands, puking her guts out.

Rushing over to her I croak out, "Are you okay?"

Surprised, she leans away from the toilet and against the wall where she wipes away the puke on the side of her beautiful lips. "Yeah. I'm fine."

"But you were throwing up. Food poisoning?"

"No…"

"You're right." I shake it off. "It's too soon for that to be the reason. Well unless it was something you ate yesterday. What did you eat yesterday? Anything different? Unusual?" Now that I think about it, I rarely see the girl eat.

Gianna ruffles her hair, which is when I notice the guilt in her eyes. "It's always the food I eat."

In an unsteady voice I ask, "Do you…do you throw up on purpose?"

I watch as she presses her lips together in refusal to answer.

Folding my arms I lean against the door fame, disapproval and disappointment on my face alike, "Do you make yourself throw up? Are you bulimic?"

"That's awfully rude of you to ask, isn't it Connor?" she growls defensively. Standing up she grabs a towel, wipes her face and tosses it in her hamper.

When she pushes past me to exit her bathroom, I grab her arm, "Hold up. I want an answer. Gianna, do you make yourself throw up?"

"I….." She shakes her head slowly, "I…I…"

"Gianna."

"Fine! Whatever! Yes!" She snatches her arm away from me. "Yes Connor, I throw up what I eat! Happy now?"

"Happy?" Confusion settling deeper and deeper. "Why would that fucking make me happy?"

"Cause I look like this." Her hand motions over her body. "It's a great diet plan! I can eat what I want, whenever I want, and look the way I want. I mean I still go to the gym and shit to stay toned, but this helps."

Appalled I let my jaw bob before I say, "You've gotta be joking."

"Well I'm not," she tries to run away again and I grab her by the arm a second time. "Let go!"

"We're not done here."

"Yes we are," her whine reminds me of MaKayla's.

"No young lady we're not."

"Young lady? What are you my dad now?"

Realizing how quickly the parental tone came out, I let her go in an attempt to dial it back. Get it and all the other emotions racing through me in check. I can't afford to blurt out something I don't mean. Not right now. "No, but speaking of, do your parents know?"

Gianna looks away.

"Well?"

"No! And there's no need for them to know!"

"Are you crazy? Yes there is! Gianna throwing up everything you eat isn't healthy for you."

"Well aren't you the poster boy for good reasoning? You know just because you don't approve doesn't make it wrong."

"You're right." I sarcastically snap. "What makes it wrong is you're hurting your body by shoving ridiculous amounts of food down your throat only to throw them up moments later. It's not healthy and it's doing serious damage to your body physically, not to mention mentally. Not to mention there are people fucking *starving*, struggling to find enough food to eat every day and you're throwing yours up like it's nothing!" The urge to mention that I'm referring to myself to drive the point home prickles along the back of my neck. I don't want to go down that path right now.

"Thank you Dr. Phil." She rolls her eyes. "You don't think I know that or the consequences of my actions? Like the life-long damage I'm causing? Because I do. I have Google. I've seen the end results. I know what I'm doing."

"Kn-Kn-Know what you're doing? Are you shitting me? What is wrong with you? Why are you so addicted to hurting yourself?"

"Because it's the only way I can feel something!" she screams in return which takes me off guard. "It's the only way I know I'm still alive and not stuck in some pathetic dream my damaged mind created! It's the only thing I can control! It's the only way I know I'm still human anymore! It's the only way I can escape from the hell my life has become! It's my sanity!"

"Being bulimic is hardly considered sane!"

"Yeah, well, this is as close as I've gotten. And why do you care anyway? It's not your problem to deal with," she tries to storm away again when I catch her by the arm once more.

This time I pull so her chest is flush with mine. "It *is* my problem to deal with. I care about you. All about you, from the fact you broke your pen in math to the fact you're praying to the porcelain god because you have no other way to control your emotions."

Even if I shouldn't care about her this way, it doesn't change that I do. I don't need this added stress to my own life that is always fucking spiraling out of control all on it's own, but something inside me needs to be in her life. I can't explain what the hell that feeling is, all I know is that it's there. I can't ignore it. I won't.

Her hands gently tug at the bottom of my shirt, eyes planted on the ground. "You...you...really care about me?"

"I do." My hand tilts her face up. "And you can't keep hurting yourself. Just because you stopped drugs doesn't mean that this is okay. Okay?" She nods as I wipe away the tear under her eye. "I know you don't wanna hear this Gianna, but we're gonna have to get you some help." She nods again before wrapping her arms around me.

Squeezing her tighter I rest my head on top of hers with my eyes shut. I knew this was gonna get complicated, I just expected it would be because of my princess. Not because the girl I'm trying to date has a list of problems money really can't solve.

Gianna's body slightly pulls back letting me see a very distinct look swirling around in her eyes. She wets her lips and slides her hands under my t-shirt, the contact just enough to make my dick start to rise in my jeans.

Not prepared in any way for where she clearly wants this make up session to go, I shake my head. "Gianna--"

"Come on Connor," she whispers out. "Let me show you how much I care about you." My mouth goes to deny the offer at the same time her hand grazes my dick on the outside of my jeans. "You want me....I know you do."

When her hand strokes me, my breath hitches while my brain begins the process of shutting out all reason. "W-W-We can't."

"Sure we can," she insists her hand now fidgeting with the button to my jeans. "I'll be gentle..."

Another wave of logic rushes out of me at the feeling of her warm fingers brushing my skin as she unzips my zipper. "No...no..."

"Yes..." Her tone is low and seductive. "Come on Connor, don't you wanna take this beautiful tongue of mine for a spin in other places? Literally. I know a good spinning trick with my tongue."

With the will power of a saint, I stop her hand seconds before it has the chance to touch my dick. "Please, don't do this to me."

"Do what?"

"Make me feel bad for saying no."

"Then don't say no."

"I have to."

"Why?"

"Because I don't--" I cut off my own voice removing her hand. "Because I can't--" With a long exhale I take a step back to zip up my jeans carefully. "Slow," is the only word that my brain can conjure.

"Slow?"

After a couple more breaths I repeat, "Slow. This. Us. That. All of it. Slow Gianna." Her jaw drops to argue and I point at her with warning, "We just kissed for the first time this week. And we still...have a lot to learn about each other, obviously."

The reference gets a small agreement from her as she wraps her arms around her stomach, the surprise of rejection still painted on her face. "But we can do that later too. We can do other stuff now....the stuff we can't do at school."

Over the last couple of years it would be a lie to say that Gianna is the first girl to throw herself at me after being told no, but I can honestly say she's the first one I've wanted to say yes to. And am on the verge of saying yes too. No. No. I have to get out of here. We have to get out of here.

"Look, right now, let's just...get to know each other with our clothes on a little more."

"Really? You wanna wait to--"

"Yeah," I cut her off, just the idea of her saying the possible next word enough for me to rethink my choice. "I really do."

"Really?"

"Really. Why does that surprise you so much?"

With a sigh she shrugs, "I've never met a guy who actually cared about me before getting me into bed. I guess I just don't understand how you know if you really like someone if you don't…well if you don't—"

"Best way to know someone is if you can tolerate them when they aren't a sexed up moaning mess." The description has me adjusting my hard on again. Poor word choice on my part.

"Sorry. I'm just used to guys sleeping with me first and asking questions later."

"Well I'm not like most guys."

I know how corny the line sounds. But it's true.

"I'm starting to see that," she whispers.

My mouth spews the truth before I can stop it. "I've learned from my mistake doing that, and it's one I'll be paying for the rest of my life."

Quickly she bites, "What's that supposed to mean? Did you rape a girl?"

"No!" Running my hand through my hair I snap, "Do I look like Goddamn rapist to you?

"No. But--"

"Look, I've made mistakes that I really don't wanna talk about right now. All that you need to know is I've learned from the past. I want to treat you better than I have past girls. I want you to be treated better than you have been in the past. I want…I want this to be different for both of us."

"Well that can't be too hard." She heads towards me, putting me in her arms again. "Especially not in the sex department."

"Why do you say that?"

My hands lightly stroke her back making her smile. "Well, since I lost my virginity at thirteen, at an after party, to a thirty year old manager of an agency my parents later signed me up to, I don't see that being too hard."

"Wow," I barely choke out.

Not that my first sexual experience was the greatest. Lost it to some college student interning at my other high school. She assumed I was a lot older than I was. I didn't tell her any different until my dick betrayed in three pump chump style. I did however vow to redeem myself with every girl after her.

75

"Not to mention any guy I slept with after that...let's just say I don't recall doing it soberly."

"So basically if you sleep with me, it'll be like your first time? Except without the pain."

"Pretty much." Gianna tries to smile and I dip my lips to touch hers softly.

Our lips linger for a moment. Pulling away I state, "Baby I definitely wanna go slow. You deserve that. You deserve to know how beautiful you are outside of the bed. So from this point on, slow okay?"

"Okay," she agrees with another peck on the lips.

"Good." My eyes glance at the clock on the wall. "Shit. We need to get back."

Gianna opens her mouth and I prepare myself for another argument. To my surprise she says, "I promised to get you back in time and I'm gonna keep that promise. Come on."

She slips out of my grip and I go to grab my backpack not exactly sure how to feel. Any time I try to dodge Gianna and go the opposite way away from her, to step back and put distance between us, something is said or done to push us back together. Dad would call the two of us together fate. But that's one lesson I never understood. How could any two people be destined to be together? How could anything be destined to happen good or bad? It sucks because the only answer he ever gave me was to have faith. Apparently he thought that was enough. I'm wondering will I ever really think that's enough too.

Chapter 9

"Damn it!" I kick the side of my tire. "Damn it!"

I continue to stare at my car that for some God awful reason won't start. Of course it won't start the day I get out of class early. No, because my life always needs some weird fucked up balance to it. Something slightly good happens so something extremely bad must happen next.

Frustrated I rub my brow unsure of how the hell I'm going to get to work or more importantly, get Mak home.

"Hey hot stuff." Gianna leans her face out her window. "Problem?"

"That's one way of putting it," I let out a deep sigh. "My car won't start."

"Ot-oh."

"And I have to be at work in a few minutes."

"Want a ride?"

"I want a jump."

"I'm all yours Baby," Gianna winks at me playfully.

Though the blue balls I've been rocking since the day she tried to give me a blow job would rather gladly take her up on her offer, I deny, "Not that kind. My car needs a jump."

"Oh," her voice dips slightly to disappointment. "Well I don't have jumper cables right now. They're somewhere in the garage, not really sure where and by the time I found them for you, you'd be late."

"Damn it," I grumble kicking the tire again.

"Calm down Incredible Hulk. Why don't you just let me give you a ride now, and I'll jump you when you get off?" My head tilts to the side as those words paint an image I wouldn't mind living in reality. She giggles and shakes her head, "Not that kind of jump."

After a short chuckle I glance back at the car seat in my back seat. I hesitate, "Thanks Gianna, but—"

"Come on Connor. It's just a ride to work. What's the big deal?"

"I—"

"Come on. You trust me enough to take you to work right?"

77

With a heavy sigh, I nod, grab my backpack and unbuckle the car seat out as quickly as possible. During the process of me slipping the car seat in the back Gianna answers her cellphone buying me a few more minutes before I have to finally confess the secret I'd planned to keep sitting on for much longer. Once it's secured, I grab my work shirt and slide into the front seat.

"No Mom. It's fine. I'll figure out something to do on my own for dinner again. It's really not a big deal." Seeing me in the seat she rushes, "I gotta go. I'll see you and Dad whenever. Bye." I part my lips to say something, but she cuts me off before I have the chance. "Where to?"

"Go out, down Deer Chase and take a right at the second light," I instruct ripping off my shirt to expose my hard earned but bruised abs.

"And what exactly do you think you're doing?" her eyes try not to wander over my body, but fail miserably.

"Changing for work."

"Oh," the heavy sigh is coated in sexual frustration. I hide my smirk. At least we're both miserable even if it is what's for the best. "Abs like that look like someone photo-shopped them."

Flattered I reply, "They're all mine Baby."

Gianna motions her fingers at the marks, "And the bruises? Where are they from?"

As my fingertips lightly graze the fading welt above my navel, I mentally relive my step father's fists landing in my stomach.

Clearing my throat I shrug, "Nowhere."

"And that one around your neck? That from nowhere too?" She points.

Unconsciously my hand shakes reaching for the area, "Yeah."

"Connor--"

"Nope." I stop the pity offer dead in its tracks. "Let it go."

"But--"

"Let it go Gianna."

In a huff, she turns where I tell her to and asks, "Where exactly do you work?"

"Voldour," I fix the collar making sure not to touch the bruise again. "It's a private preschool."

"You work at a preschool?" She tries to stifle her laugh. "Seriously?"

"Why is that funny?"

"You're an 18 year old guy who willingly works with children?"

"No. I'm the handyman. I fix most of the problems they have and if I can't they hire someone who can. Do you have a problem with children?"

Gianna pauses at the stop sign. "No. One of the deals with completing my last rehab program was that I had to do volunteer work, so I helped out teaching dance to toddlers and preschoolers. It was actually kind of fun."

A small surge goes through my body and for just a moment I feel relief. Maybe this whole thing won't be a giant disaster. Maybe it'll be a minor one.

"Do you have to work every day?"

"Every afternoon from when I get out of school until they close at 6:30. Sometimes I have to pull in an extra hour or so after they close. I work weekends when necessary. Lawn maintenance usually."

"Not your typical after school job huh?"

"No. I make much more and don't have to flip burgers."

She grins and asks, "Where to now Mr. Fix It?"

"You'll see the school up here on the right."

Gianna continues down the road seeing the entrance from the parking lot by the school. Putting on her blinker she questions, "What's the car seat for? Did you take it home to fix it over night or something?"

Pressing my lips together, I reach for my ringing cell phone, which just so happens to be work, "Hello."

Nelly softly asks, "Running a little late?"

"Yeah. Sorry. My car wouldn't start. And I couldn't find anyone to give me a jump. Thankfully my girlfriend could give me a ride."

The word is out on the table before I've had time to mentally prepare myself. Shit. That wasn't...that wasn't supposed to come out like that. I don't even know if we're a couple. I mean, the kind of couple who should say they are a couple. I just...fuck. Why did I say that?

"Oh that's okay," Nelly sighs. "Glad you got a ride. I was just calling to let you know MaKayla has been complaining she doesn't feel good since she woke up from her nap and acting a bit out of the ordinary. Clingier. So when you get here, if you want to check on her go right ahead. I won't be at front because we're short-handed *again* today. Helping in infants."

"I'll make sure to get back there immediately."

"Are you close?"

"Very," I smile.

"Hopefully, I'll see you shortly then Connor," she sighs and hangs up.

Once I've hung up Gianna ponders out loud, "Who was that?"

"The office. They know that due to school sometimes I'm late and just wondered was that the case. They're really nice and understanding when it comes to my situation."

"And what situation is that exactly?" she asks pulling up in front of the white brick building.

Dodging the question, I open my door, "I get off at 6:30, well, I mean I should. If anything changes, I'll give you a call. Do you think you can be back here by then?"

"Totally. I have nothing else to do. Maybe I'll just go down the road and do a little shopping. Oooo! Maybe I'll grab you a new pair of jeans. Like a pair that hugs your ass."

With darted eyebrows I shake my head, "No. Don't do that." Gianna giggles and I plant a quick kiss on her lips, slightly addicted to the action. "But have fun."

"You have a good day," she states before I close the door and rush off to work.

As soon as I'm clocked in Nelly hands me my list of duties for the day, "Didn't know you were that close. I was just about to step away."

"Surprisingly not as late as I thought I was gonna be."

"Just a minute," she struggles to stand. I slide around the desk to help her up and she says, "I feel so bad for Mak. I went down there to give one of the girl's a bathroom break and she just didn't want me to go. Rough morning?"

Rough night is more like it. If my prick step father would've just left quietly last night I wouldn't have had to toss his ass in a fight in the middle of the night.

"A little. She really didn't want to go to school today, but I told her if Daddy has to go to school so does she."

Nelly lets my hand go and points. "Well go make her feel better, before you get busy."

I head down the hall until I reach the very end where I peek in on her class. Luckily for me she's easy to find. She's sitting with a group of friends at a table full of crayons and coloring pages.

Watching, I give her a second to see if she'll notice me before I walk in to see her. When she doesn't, I open the door and wave to her favorite teacher, Ms. Nelson, who is hanging up art work around the room.

Instantly MaKayla looks up and yells, "Daddy!"

"Hi Princess!" I swiftly swoop her into a big hug. "How are you?"

"I wanna go home," she pouts in my arms, her head on my shoulder and her little pinky in her mouth.

"Not right now Princess. At the end of the day like always," I stroke her hair as I wave to a few of her friends, who are trying to get my attention.

"Now," she whines, further evidence that the fight last night took a hard toll on her. Just a few more months before I can move us out. Move us far away from that bastard and my mother who can't seem to do the right thing for her son like I do the right thing for my daughter.

"No Mak. Later."

"But Daddy--"

"Daddy has to work Mak."

Tears fill her eyes and she sniffles, "But Daddy..."

My heart aches in my chest and I hold her closer. "I know Princess. I'm sorry."

"Are we still having ice cream?" Her small hand pulls at my collar.

"I don't know Baby. No promises, but I'll try okay?"

Mak sniffles again, "Okay."

"I need you to be a big girl for Daddy. You have a big job to do! What do I always say?"

"Learning is a big job and only Mak can do it!" She says excited.

"Exactly. Now, can I have a kiss before you go play with your friends?"

She places her tiny lips on my cheek, giggles, and slides down my body like a fire pole. "I love you."

"I love you," I coo back. "Be good for Ms. Nelson."

Ms. Nelson walks over to us and leans her body against the teacher desk in the front of the classroom. While Kendall has always made a point to hit on me, Ms. Nelson has always tried to be a friend. A shoulder to lean on. An ear to vent to even though I refuse to bitch out loud about my problems. The gesture isn't lost on me. I just choose not to use it. "It's been a rough day Connor. She's just been crying a lot more than she ever has. I've actually held her a lot. She's not rocking a fever or anything."

"She didn't sleep well last night. Usually when that happens she still wakes up ready to spend the day with you and just takes an extra hard nap, so I don't know what to say. You think I should be worried?"

Ms. Nelson offers me a soft smile. "Nah. Kids have good days and bad just like the rest of us. If this turns into an on-going thing we can talk about deeper issues, but in my opinion I think she just wants some Daddy time."

"I will make sure she has that tonight," I assure. "Thanks Ms. Nelson."

"Any time."

"Stop it," she gives me a playful flirt, a hair toss, and another smile.

After giving Mak another look as she colors the cow pink and purple, I say, "Well I'm heading out. Got work to do. You have a good afternoon Ms. Nelson."

"You too," she waves before rushing off to break up a fight between a pair of boys.

Fortunately for me when 6:30 rolls around I've finished and can pick up MaKayla on time rather than have her wander to the office to wait with Nelly.

"Daddy you're early!" Mak exclaims as I open her classroom door.

"No Princess, just on time," I reply grabbing her backpack.

Extending my hand for her to take I'm not shocked when she shakes her head. "No. Up Daddy."

"Mak..."

"Please," she adds and lifts her arms in the air.

Before we leave her classroom where Ms. Nelson is stacking the last of the chairs, I pull Mak up and carry her out the door, thanking her teacher seconds before the door shuts. On our way towards the front, Kendall rounds the corner right into us.

"Connor!" Her voice is startled. "I'm surprised I actually caught you."

I adjust Mak on my hip and say, "You did. Need something?"

"I was wondering if you wanted to grab a bite, since we're getting off at the same time and everything."

"Uh...I'm flattered, seriously, but..."

"But what?"

"I can't. I...I have a girlfriend."

"Oh! I didn't know! I mean if I had I wouldn't have asked you. I mean I—"

"I know. We just started dating and—"

"You don't have to explain." She puts her hands in the air. "Really I just—"

"I know." The pause is long enough for the sentence to be concluded. "Sorry Kendall, but I--"

"Need to go." She disappointedly nods. "Don't keep your girlfriend waiting. Have a good night."

"You too," I nod in return, turn to walk away, but decide to turn around. "Hey Kendall."

"Yeah?" She turns around from going back to her classroom.

"Just know that I really like you as a person. You're something special," I smile slightly, which makes her smile too.

Strolling away I let my attention turn to Mak who states, "Daddy has a girlfriend."

Damn it. That's at least the second time today I didn't think that statement through.

"Baba daddy. I need Baba," she whines as I approach the front desk area to clock out. Sitting her on the counter, I plop her backpack down beside her to dig out the bear.

83

Nelly's face leans towards her, "Did someone have a rough day?"

Handing Mak her bear she snuggles it close. She pokes her bottom lip out and turns to Nelly.

"Poor thing." Nelly gives her back a soft stroke. "Was someone just a little sad all day?"

"I missed my daddy," Mak whines and tugs for me to pick her back up. After clocking out, I zip the bag, and lift her back into my arms. Immediately her thumb goes into her mouth, "I need my Daddy."

"And now you have him," Nelly sighs softly. "So all better?"

After giving her a nod, she slides her thumb back out. "Can we get ice cream now daddy?"

"Mak, Daddy's car is broken, so I—"

"But Daddy!" she screams, the making of a tantrum clear as day. I really don't need that today. Then again. I don't ever really need a tantrum in my life.

"Mak--"

"But Daddy!" She starts crying burying her face on my chest.

"Night Nelly," I mouth while her tears get louder.

Through muffled bawling she continues demanding ice cream and cuddles, the combination of demands so heartbreaking it feels like she's reaching in my chest and twisting sharply. With both my arms cradling her close, I continue on my path to Gianna's car where she's leaning against the driver's side door.

Puzzled she raises an eyebrow. "Yeah, I don't think you're supposed to take them home…That's called kidnapping. And I like you Connor. I do. But I'm not sure a Bonnie and Clyde relationship is what I'm looking for."

"You really think that's funny, don't you?"

"It is," she huffs playfully. "Some of my best work."

"And you had such promise before…"

"Oh come on. That was so funny."

"If you say so Catwoman. This one actually belongs to me." I kiss my daughter's tear stained cheek.

"You have a…" The sentence seems to drop. "A…a…well a…"

"Yeah." My face tries to force a smile, but struggles. "Hence the car seat."

Speechless, she just watches. MaKayla's fit continues until she's violently coughing and kicking, which is when I try shushing her by running my fingers through her hair.

Finally finding words she asks, "What's wrong with her?"

"She wants me to take her for ice cream because I usually do if she has a really rough day, but my car's in the school's parking lot and by the time we get to the car, finally jump it and get it started, I'll need to get her home and settle down for dinner and so on," I explain to Gianna before leaning my head to whisper in Mak's ear. "It's not that Daddy doesn't wanna take you. It's just that Daddy can't."

The tears begin to fly into overflow mode when Gianna speaks up, "We can all go."

"What?" I stop rubbing her back, which makes her pause mid cry.

"We can all go," a deep sigh escapes her. "All three of us."

"But—"

"Yay!" MaKayla cries out wiping her tears away. "Ice cream! Ice cream Daddy!"

Quickly, I try again, "But—"

"If it's okay with your Daddy I would love to get ice cream together," Gianna softly speaks to my daughter, wiping away tears off her cheek. "You are much too pretty to be so sad. I bet you have a really pretty smile. Can I see?"

MaKayla's face bursts into a smile. A genuine one. Immediately I know this fight is over. We're going to have to go.

Now in her bright, cheerful voice she bounces in my arms, "Can we Daddy? Oh please can we have ice cream? Please can we have ice cream with your girlfriend?"

One word. Multiple slips. And the timing. The timing just keeps getting worse with it. If talking about my child won't be enough stress, having 'the talk' about where this relationship is going and can't go, will just be the cherry on top of this Goddamn day.

"Princess..." I start in my stern father tone, which forces the tears in her eyes to return. Clearly she needs this. She needs time away from the apartment. Time where she feels safe with me. I fucking hate that her own home isn't safe for her. With a heavy sigh I brush the hair out of her eyes, kiss her forehead, and nod. "Okay. We can have ice cream, but I really don't like to eat ice cream before dinner."

"Let's stop someplace where we can get both," Gianna suggests, a sincere tone of happiness in it. Unsure of what she's trying to do or even thinking for that matter, she says, "You know what? Why don't we go to Pizzaland? There's all you can eat pizza and ice cream plus playscapes and games we can play together. How does that sound?"

Expensive. That's how that sounds. In a defeated whisper I argue, "Gianna I can't really afford that."

"My treat." She unlocks the car doors.

"Come on Gianna, you don't have to. Seriously."

"I want to." For a moment her eyes just stay planted in mine.

In a hushed tone I fight, "You really don't have to."

"I want to take my boyfriend and his daughter to dinner. I think I reserve that right as the girlfriend, don't you?"

See. Knew this was going to come back on me again.

"Gianna--"

"Stop fighting Connor and let's get this little Princess something to eat," she snips before leaning over to talk to MaKayla again. "What do you think? Think we should go get some dinner and ice cream and play?"

"Yay!" Mak squeals. "I like Daddy's girlfriend!"

"I do too," I say on a light chuckle at the shift in attitude. Thankful to have her smiling instead of crying, I drop the fear that's lingering about this turning into a disaster. I'm sure it will. But for now, for Mak's sake at the very least, I need to enjoy this. "MaKayla can you say hi to Gianna?"

"Hi!" She squeaks. "I like that you're my Daddy's girlfriend!"

"I like that I'm his girlfriend too," she giggles in return before opening the back door. "And it's nice to meet you MaKayla."

"Mak," I inform her. "You can call her Mak."

"Daddy calls me Princess," Mak announces loudly.

"You are the prettiest princess I have ever seen," Gianna's compliment sounds so beautiful that I can't resist what I do next. Leaning over I softy push my lips against hers unexpectedly. She welcomes the abrupt kiss with a brief touch of our tongues. She pulls back and stares in my eyes again, refilling the bucket of anxiousness. I know this will change things between us. Whatever things are about to change, but I hope I don't lose her as a result. I understand if I do. Asking your girlfriend to understand you have a child isn't easy, especially when you haven't graduated high school yet. "Ready?"

"Yeah." I clear my throat. "Let's get you buckled in Mak."

"And ice cream!" She energetically giggles again.

Thankful to see her in a better state, I put her in her car seat with a smile, while Gianna looks over my shoulder. Under her breath she nervously questions, "You sure it's secure in there? You sure that's it's safe? Can she unbuckle herself?"

I click her last buckle, drop Mak's backpack at her feet, and turn so my face meets Gianna's. "It's fine. She's fine."

"You sure?" The concern has my hands landing on her hips. "Do you wanna drive? I mean--"

"Gianna," I cut her off slightly thankful to see this side kick in versus the opposite that I'm sure will catch up with me soon. "We're fine. Just hungry. So unless you've changed your mind, you wanna head us that direction? Mak didn't eat much today and is probably starving."

"Her Daddy didn't either." She pokes my chest.

Once Mak's door is shut I state, "Money's tight. My daughter eats first and if there's food after that I'll eat."

"Tonight you're both eating." Gianna lifts her mouth up to mine for a peck on the lips. "And so am I." Skeptical I raise my eyebrows. "And keeping it down." Seeing the relief on my face she says, "I was waiting to tell you about it, but after...after that day, I did a little online research and found a good therapist to start seeing and we're working on some things."

"Do your parents know?"

"No," she bluntly remarks. "They'd have to see me more than 10 minutes a week to know that." Without giving me a chance to rebuttal, Gianna opens her car door. "Let's go."

I head for my side, but stop. "One more thing Gianna?"

"Yeah?"

"We can't talk about Mak's m-o-m or that situation in front of her. I'll explain, eventually, but not in front of her okay?"

"Okay." She nods. "Understood."

The three of us head to the pizza place with me primarily asking Mak how her day was and Gianna commenting where she sees fit. She takes time to ask my daughter questions that excite her and keep her mood joyful. At dinner we get three buffets, spend time chasing Mak around the indoor playground and racing her down the slide. I go back for seconds and thirds, leaving the two of them together allowing me to watch giggle fits and what it would be like if Mak had her mother in her life. If she had a female who cared enough to put her first. The longing to give my daughter what I can't affects my appetite each time it hits me. Pushing my plate away, I continue staring as Gianna pulls Mak's hair into a high pony tail. From the reaction on my daughter's face her entire day has been turned around as she motions her hands for Gianna to lift her up. Even if I don't deserve the happiness that's pumping through the air, my innocent little girl does.

The two of them walk over to me, both beaming. Gianna looks down at me, "You okay?"

"Yup," I reply with a nod forcing a smile on my face.

"Daddy see my pony!" Her tiny head wiggles back and forth.

"It's beautiful. Did you tell Gianna thank you."

"She did," Gianna answers. "Great manners. Very polite. Very sweet. But we both agree...it's ice cream time."

"Ice cream daddy!"

"Alright, alright." I stand and escort them over to the dessert area, Gianna still holding Mak, while my hand rests on Gianna's lower back.

We look like a family. We sound like a family. We feel like a family. Doing my best to shake the solicitous swarming in my mind, I order us sundaes while the two of them pretend to fight over the better flavor of ice cream. As I grab our two bowls and let Gianna grab the other I can't help but notice the few over opinionated looks we receive. It's normal for me. The disapproval. The disgust. The judgment over being a teenage father. It wasn't my fucking choice. But that rarely makes people or at least strangers any more understanding. Typically I ignore it and let it roll off my shoulders, but tonight the glaring eyes added to the shit storm of a day it's been are too much.

"Daddy," Mak whines. "Eat your ice cream."

"Daddy's full Princess," I insist. "But you finish yours all up, so we can get you home. You're gonna need a bath."

"No bath," Mak pouts licking her fingers.

"You're sticky."

"No."

"It's not up for debate MaKayla. A bath when we get home."

Her ice cream covered mouth scrunches and the creation of another tantrum caused by sleep deprivation begins in her eyes.

"I bet you have the best bath toys," Gianna joins the conversation distracting her. When Mak nods she questions, "How about you show them to me? Does that sound like a plan?"

"Yeah!" Mak squeaks, ice cream dripping down her hands. "I show you my bath toys in the bath!"

Firmly I state, "Gianna."

In the same tone she replies, "Connor."

"MaKayla!" My daughter adds with another round of giggles.

I surrender the discussion for the moment knowing once we get in the car and Mak passes out from the car ride, I can explain to her why bath time with the three of us isn't just a bad idea. It's not even a fucking option.

On the ride home instead of to my car, MaKayla tells the strangest story about something that happened to her at school until she passes out in her car seat, which has its obvious benefit of her getting extra rest and not having to worrying about her staying up late. The rest of the ride, aside from directions being given on the route to take, we make awkward small talk about school clearly trying to avoid the topic we both know we need to discuss.

When Gianna finally pulls into my apartment complex with a very cautious look on her face she stutters to ask, "D-D-Do you need me to help you up the stairs?"

"No," I quickly reject. "I can handle it."

"Are you sure? I mean between carrying her, her car seat, your backpack, her backpack, and her new stuffed animals, I think it's a little much. Why don't you just let me help you carry them up the stairs?" Gianna parks in my normal parking space.

I want to tell her how I'm worried not just about her safety but the safety of her vehicle. How the likelihood that someone tries to jack it as soon as we're out of it is high. "Gianna I—"

"Connor, stop being stubborn." She pulls her keys out of the ignition. "Grab your daughter and your backpack. I'll get the rest."

Exhausted, any fight left in me for the argument or any argument for that matter is gone. I nod, and do as asked before leading us up to the apartment where I hear silence, an uncomfortable sound as far as I'm concerned. Putting the key in the door, I'm startled by the sight of Paul on the couch red eyed with a drunken expression, and my mother beside him legs apart, obviously drunk too, but thankfully passed out.

"Well hey Junior," he sneers, rolling his head to me as Gianna slides in behind me. "Come back for another round?" After a chuckle he scratches the scruff on his face, "Didn't get enough damage yesterday? Decide you needed some more licks?"

Cradling Mak closer to me, I make sure my body stands in a protective position to defend Gianna if necessary. I won't let him hurt her either. He'll leave here in a body bag and me in handcuffs before I'd let him lay a finger on her. On a low growl I ask, "What the fuck are you doing here? Didn't you get paid in pussy yesterday?"

"That I did Junior." He wags his finger at me. "Felt like a double dose this month, but now that you mention it…I've got payment to collect elsewhere. Tell your mother I'll see her same time next month." Getting up he gives Gianna a dirty glance that flexes my body further. To my surprise she pushes her body into mine. I never wanted her to feel the fear I do. That my daughter goes through. She shouldn't have too. She shouldn't be here. But she is. And I won't let anything fucking happen to either of them. "Who's the bitch behind you? She's a looker."

"Don't even fucking think about it," I growl, clutching Mak tighter. "What I'd do to you wouldn't even compare to what I've done before."

"Threatin' me Junior?"

"Promising six feet under if you so much as look at my girlfriend the wrong way."

Paul smirks as he slides his leather coat on him. "Touchy touchy junior. Don't you worry your fucking island trash brain over it. I don't do jail bait."

Knowing how much I wanna sock him in the mouth for the insult, but more desperate to have him away from the women in my life I'll most likely die trying to protect, I let the comment go.

"If you two lovebirds will excuse me, I've got money to make." I take a step back, keeping Gianna pressed to me and out of his grip. He opens the door with a smug smirk, "Remember to wear a rubber this time. Wouldn't want you to have any more brats you can't fucking afford."

As soon as the door is closed, I shutter him away, and glance at my mother who is showing her choice of panties to the world in her pink mini skirt. Nothing about this day has gone the way it should've. If my father was here he would quote some ancient proverb about fate or destiny, but how is this either of those things? Fate and destiny both imply something *good* is happening or in the making, doesn't it?

"This way," I grumble and head down the hall towards my bedroom with Gianna in close proximity to me. I allow her to open my bedroom door to my thankfully neat room despite Mak's hard attempts to undo that by insisting every section of our room is a different magical kingdom. She closes the door behind me as I gently lay MaKayla down to change her into her pajamas. I know she's sticky among other things, but after our day she deserves to stay asleep.

In a whisper Gianna asks, "So this is where both of you sleep?" Receiving a nod she gives the room another look around. "Not really spacious."

"Well not all of us are as fortunate as you," I whisper out, somewhat bitterly as I begin to change Mak.

"Sorry. That wasn't meant to sound bitchy."

Realizing she's right and the combination of being annoyed, sensitive about the subject, and on edge that the people I care about most may all be under one roof, but aren't safe, forces out an apology, "I'm sorry. It wasn't."

Gianna leans against the edge of our dresser. She says in an unsure tone, "Please don't take this the wrong way, especially because I am no child expert, she doesn't seem like she has a lot of room to play."

The feeling of irritation starts stirring again. "She doesn't."

"I thought that was something children needed."

"It is," I snip back, tucking Mak underneath the blanket once she's in a clean pair of panties and a princess night gown. Shooting her an unpleasant look I explain, "But, I work with what I'm given. I usually move her toys to the living room, so she can have that kind of space. However you witnessed what lies on the other side of this door, so that is not always a logical option." Receiving another nod, I turn back around, kiss Mak goodnight, and whisper an 'I love you'.

For a moment I forget that Gianna is even in the room as I watch my angel resting happily from a dream come true day for her. She had everything she's ever wanted for a few hours. That joy. That excitement. That love. All of it worth the rest of the fucking shit I had to endure for the rest of the day. Everything I do is worth it for her.

Coming back to the reality that Gianna is still in my room, I turn on my heels. "Thanks for helping me up the stairs with my stuff. I can walk you back down now that she's tucked in. Are you ready to go home?"

Her eyebrows raise as she softly ponders, "Would you like me to go home?"

"Is that a joke? I know you don't wanna stay here."

"How do you know that?"

"Because I don't even wanna stay here."

"Well, maybe I do." She turns the lock on my door.

Not sure I can handle sexual frustration with the rest of the days unstable ground, I quickly say, "Gianna, you know we can't—"

"I'm not trying to do anything like that. I swear." She lets out a heavy sigh, moves the hair out of her gorgeous face that has less make up on than I remember her having just a week ago, and makes sure to keep her eyes on mine. "I just figured maybe…maybe you didn't wanna be alone tonight? Maybe we could cuddle or something?"

Skeptical I lift my eyebrows. "You wanna cuddle?"

"That's what couples do right?" I give her another doubting look. "I don't know Connor!" The change in volume stirs Mak. Immediately she calms her voice back down, "I don't know if real couples cuddle or not. Or can share a bed without having sex, but can we try it? Is it so wrong to wanna spend the night with you? My jaw starts ticking, but I don't answer. She shouldn't stay the night. She should've never came up those fucking stairs. Her life was put at risk. Mak's life in danger is enough on my conscious. I don't need hers too. "Maybe I stay the night and we lie together? I can give you two a ride in the morning…"

On a deep sigh, knowing if she gave us a ride it would be easier than dealing with my hung over mother, I start to agree when Mak whimpers in her sleep. My eyes cut over just as she smiles in her sleep. I turn back to Gianna, "I don't know. I mean if Mak wakes up and you're here then that might—"

"Give her hope that I'm here to stay?" I don't reply. "I understand where you're coming from, but how will she get used to me if not given the chance? Because guess what Connor? I'm not going anywhere. This doesn't scare me away any more than what you found out about me scares you. I'm still here. I'm still standing in front of you, so let me."

Baffled and worn out I drop on the edge of my bed, "Why Gianna?"

"Why what?"

"Why are you still standing here? Most girls--"

"I have been most girls and I know you know that." When I threaten a small smirk she pushes. "I want to be a part of her world, because that's being a part of your world. I care about you. A lot."

Hearing her say the words twists that small fraction of hope inside of me until it's wedged back exactly where it needs to be. To that place where I need it to be to get out of bed in the morning. After I clear my throat I motion her body to come over to mine. When she's standing in front of me, I pull her so she's sitting in my lap. "Alright you stay the night, but can you save all the hard hitting questions until tomorrow?"

She places a small kiss on my cheek before she smiles. "Definitely." Unsure if I'm making the right choice or not, I prepare to suit up for battle on the war inside once more when she pushes her lips sweetly on mine. The startle from me is brief as she places a hand on my cheek like a flag of victory for calming back down at the same time her tongue touches mine. Apparently tranquility can be found under her tongue. When she pulls back, a humming through my body has wiped out the last wave of insecurity over the situation. "Now...do you mind letting me borrow a t-shirt and boxers to sleep in?"

With a crooked smile I nod, "I can do that."

She stands up and I grab her an old white t-shirt and a pair of clean boxers, thankful I did laundry recently. As soon as they are in her hands I open my mouth to explain where the bathroom is when she starts kicking off her shoes.

"What are you doing?"

"Changing," she hums in return. Before I can insist she changes in the other room, her top is off and I'm staring at a perfect pair of tits propped up in a black bra. My dick starts to swell at the first pair of boobs I've seen since this sick, sad, internal vow of celibacy. Knowing I should look away, I swallow the lump of excitement from just the glance of her like this. Gianna places a hand on her hip. "You're staring."

"You're fucking gorgeous," my mouth mumbles all on its own.

"Thank you," she replies and slides my t-shirt on covering the blindingly beautiful sight. "For both compliments." Confused I tilt my head to the side until she points to my package.

I turn on a groan and adjust my hard on. "Sorry. It's been awhile..."

"How long?"

Pulling off my own shirt, I give her a sideways smile over my bare shoulder. "Thought we agreed to save all the hard hitting questions until the morning?"

Gianna rolls her eyes and begins to unbutton her jeans. I drag my eyes away before the sight of her in a thong undoes years of self-restraint in seconds. Focusing on myself, I grab a pair of basketball shorts off the floor and change into them. When I'm finished I turn around to see my girlfriend, leaned against the dresser in my clothes, making me long for something I know that's not a real possibility.

"So…bed time?" She questions pointing to the space on the other side of Mak, who has rolled over, her bear in a choke hold and her thumb in her mouth.

"I actually have some math homework I need to do, but you can crash if you want."

"Well since we have the same math teacher, why don't I just do my homework with you? They were just book problems right?"

"Yeah."

Swiftly she yanks up my backpack and dangles it in front of me. In a playful tone she says, "First, theater partners. Now Math partners. Wherever shall we end up next?"

I know she's just being playful, but I can't keep myself from wondering the same damn thing.

Chapter 10

The next morning, I'm rudely awakened to the sound of banging on my bedroom door and a rattling door handle. Through my own groans I manage to force myself to sit up, stretch for a moment, and glance at both Gianna and my daughter who are still sleeping. Rubbing the sleep out of my eye, I manage to smile at Mak, who was nestled between us, and the way she's curled into Gianna like this is how we wake up every morning. Another harsh banging has them stirring and me moving quickly before the sound ruins everyone's morning.

I unlock and open the door to see my mother with a livid expression. On a yawn I bite, "Can I help you?"

"Why the hell is your door locked?" she snaps her coffee cup in a death clutch, nails clinking the sides.

"Safety," my raspy voice comments. Unexpectedly, she shoves the door and exposes the view I woke up to.

"And who the hell is that?" My mother raises her voice. "Is that a girl in your room, Connor?"

Gently nudging her forward to shut the door behind me, I state, "I don't really feel like talking about this right now."

"Oh we're going to talk about this right now," she bites bitterly. "In the kitchen now."

Annoyed, I follow her into the kitchen where I immediately go to the washroom to grab Mak something to wear.

"Why is there a girl in your bedroom, Connor?"

"Why was Paul here yesterday?"

"Don't change the subject!" Tossing around clothes I search for something more spring friendly than her jeans she complains are too hot. "Why is there a girl in your bed?"

"She spent the night," I nonchalantly answer pulling out jeans for me and a short sleeve sweater dress for Mak. Knowing she'll probably need leggings to go underneath, I start digging again. "Now why was Paul here?"

"No." Her heel covered foot stomps the kitchen floor. "This conversation isn't over. What the hell makes you think you can have girls sleeping over?"

Not in the mood to start my day this way, but having no choice, I toss our clothes over my bare shoulder and lean against the kitchen counter. "I'm gonna go with the fact I'm eighteen—"

"Exactly Connor! You're *only* eighteen!"

"Yeah. Eighteen carrying the weight and responsibility of a thirty year old! It's about time I start reaping the benefits of my actions." There's no way I'm about to fucking reap the benefits of my actions. I'm not stupid, but am tired and in no mood for her to feel like playing parent.

"Have you thought about the *consequences* of your actions?"

"You mean from having a girl sleep in my bed? Yeah Mom. I've thought about the fact my sheets are going to smell like sugar and vanilla for the next few days."

"You know what I mean smart ass."

"Do I?"

"I know you do."

"Just say it. Ask that question the way you really want."

"Sex Connor. Have you thought about the consequence of having sex again? And if you have, which I'm thinking you haven't by your not giving a damn attitude, have you forgotten that your daughter should serve as a reminder of why you should keep that thing between your legs there and not in someone?"

"Look, Mother of the Year, I think about that every day, every minute with every fucking decision I make. Everything I do, every choice I make, good, bad, difficult, and painful I make for that little girl who only has one fucking parent. And not that it's any of your damn business, but I didn't have sex with her. I haven't had sex since I became a father and until I'm comfortable with the thought of another kid popping into my life I'm not going to. I'm not as dumb as you fucking think I am."

Slowly becoming more defeated with each passing sentence she huffs, "Then why'd you let her stay the night? You think MaKayla is going to have a healthy reaction? She's going to get confused and start to call her mom and—"

"And what's the big deal with that?" I interrupt, which makes her choke on her coffee. I know what the big deal is. I'm already in over my head with the choices I keep making in regards to Gianna and I's relationship in direct correlation to me and Mak's. Mak doesn't need to get attached or her hopes nestled in someone so understandable, so selfish, so used to not thinking about anything other than her small line of vision, but there's something there. There's a way Mak looks at her that she's never looked at anyone else. The same way she gets lost in her princess movies. How can I just yank that away? Especially with this nagging feeling that I'm more tempted to call it love every time I look into her eyes too long. Fuck. Why is life so Goddamn complicated?

My mother stutters, "Wh-Wh-What's the big deal?"

"What if this is the girl for me and this is going to be Mak's stepmother?"

"Stepmother?!" She shrieks.

What the fuck am I saying? Which part of this is true anymore and which is for shock value?

"Stepmother?!"

"Shouldn't they both be given the chance to slowly make that adjustment? Shouldn't Mak get to transition slowly into a new life where she has two parents?"

Frustrated my mother clinks her nails against her cup growling through gritted teeth, "I don't think this is a good idea Connor. Any of it. Not slumber parties! Not the idea of you feeling you're ready for that kind of commitment! None of it! You're only 18 for Christ sake! Just no Connor! I don't think any of this a good fucking idea."

"Noted. Can I go now?"

"No!" She reaches for my arm, which is when I notice a path of bruises up hers. "You need to think about this Connor! You need to be aware of what you're doing!"

"Why don't you take your own Goddamn advice huh?" I turn her arm over and point to the marks. "Why don't you think about the guys you bring into this apartment and the damage it has done and is doing to your own fucking child?"

"Excuse you. I am a grown woman," her voice raises. "And I know how to handle these situations!"

"Do you?"

"Yes."

"Do you really?"

"Yes, Connor."

"Then why do I have bruises all over my body because of the white trash you married?" I point to the marks covering my stomach, which is when I watch my mother's body cringe. Tilting my head back, I point to the ring around my neck. "Do you see this? Do you see this?" She looks away and I pull her a little closer and harshly point again, "Look at it! Look at it Mom! This is from where your piece of shit husband threw me into the wall by my neck—"

"I know."

"By my neck!" I reiterate. "You're worried about a girl falling asleep in my bed and Mak being traumatized from a new person waking up with us, yet you couldn't give a shit less about the fact your own son is fucking breaking. Death a realistic option every time I step foot in the door. You're worried about me moving on to a healthier situation instead of the fact I have to lie to my own daughter, your granddaughter, about how I got the marks, not to mention my teachers, and my bosses because if I were to explain to them the kind of environment I actually live in, they might try to take my own child away. You call putting your son through this being a grown woman?"

My mother's voice warns, "Connor..."

"Which part of that is the adult way to handle life?"

She threatens again, "Connor don't..."

"You haven't been a fucking parent since Dad died."

Her hand flies across my face, the sting sharp. "Don't! You don't have any idea what that was like!"

"I was there too!" I shout, tears filling my eyes. "I watched him die too! And I have to live every day without him just like you, so don't fucking tell me I don't have any idea what that's like."

A sob chokes her voice and the hand holding the mug shakes severely.

Swallowing the lack of self-control that has spun out of control, I sigh in a softer volume, "Next time you approach me with some bullshit about not having a girl sleep over because it might...MIGHT...hurt my daughter, try to remember this fucking conversation. Excuse me."

I push past her, the sound of her sniffles coursing through me. She didn't deserve all that. But you know what? Neither did I. Annoyed I sigh, I make a note to smooth everything over after I've had more sleep, food, and passed the econ test that I'm not so sure about.

When I open my bedroom door, I'm not only surprised at the sound of the music pumping through it, but Gianna, braiding Mak's hair, the two of them giggling. Leaning against the door frame, I watch for just a minute as Mak sings loudly into the hairbrush. The sight of the two of them looking so natural and so real feels like a double edged sword to the ribs. What am I supposed to do? Rip Mak away from the first mother figure to ever enter her world because it might not last or keep her around until she gets bored of playing house and she breaks both of our hearts.

"Daddy!" Mak finally notices me lurking. "See my princess braids! I have princess braids!"

"You do." I step into the room and close the door. "And you look beautiful Angel."

"I know!" She croaks as Gianna turns to look at me.

"Had some things in my purse. Figured, why not? Doubt you know how to braid her hair."

"I'm a headband kind of dad, what can I say?" She smiles in return and I curiously ask, "When did you get your purse? I thought you left that in the car last night."

"I did. I got it while you were asleep."

"You snuck out of the apartment in the middle of the night? Alone?" my parental tone kicks in.

With a displeased look she raises an eyebrow, "I am not your daughter. Please do not talk to me like that."

"That's Daddy's grumpy voice," Mak adds.

"It's not a nice voice for sure," Gianna replies to her before looking back up at me. "I'm a big girl Connor. I can walk to my car on my own."

"It's not safe."

"And yet here I am," her sarcasm joins the pile of shit I'm not in the mood for this morning. "I'm okay. I appreciate the concern."

"I hate the idea of something happening to you, especially if I could've prevented it. Could you just wait for me next time?"

"There's gonna be a next time?" She excitedly asks.

"Yay! More sleepovers!" Mak giggles hopping on the bed.

This is the drawback to talking so damn much. Words just fly out of my mouth without waiting for my brain to finish processing it. I need more sleep. I need more time to think about all this shit. I need...I need...I need my dad.

"Let's get you dressed for school," Gianna speaks up. "Looks like your daddy brought you something to wear."

"I don't wanna wear that dress!" Mak pouts folding her arms.

"Makayla--"

"You sure?" Gianna cuts me off. "I think that's the prettiest princess dress I've ever seen."

"Really?" Mak's eyes pop out of her small head. "Ever? Ever?"

"Ever. Ever. Ever," she exaggerates with hand motions. "If you're not gonna wear it, I sure will!"

"It's too small for you silly," Mak insists bouncing across the bed and into my arms. "Daddy, I'm hungry."

"Me too," Gianna adds rising to her feet. "What if we all get ready for school and then grab something quick? My treat."

Not enjoying the increasing feeling like a charity case I sigh, "We have food we can eat here."

"Good." She folds her arms across her stomach. "You'll need it I'm sure, but as for now, I'm thinking pancakes?"

"Pancakes!" Mak squirms for joy in my arm. Her hands fly to my cheeks and she squeezes. "Pancakes Daddy!"

With a smile I press a kiss on her forehead. "I heard. But this is a special treat. Tomorrow, back to normal. Okay?"

"Yes Daddy." She touches my nose. "I have to potty."

"Come on." I open the door. "Let's go potty, get you changed, and your teeth brushed before pancakes and school." Excited she nods and I shoot Gianna a look, "I don't...I don't have anything for you to wear."

She points to my dresser, "I do." My eyes cut to a pair of jeans laid out with long sleeve black top. "Always prepared."

Mumbling under my breath I shake my head walking out of the room, "Of course you are..."

After we're all dressed, we take Mak for pancakes, before dropping her off, skipping all of first period. The two of us park with just enough time to give each other a quick peck before rushing to opposite ends of the school in fear of being tardy. Thankfully, my econ test requires more of my focus than anything else leaving no time for me to dwell on what I haven't said and explained or what I haven't put a stop to and should. As soon as lunch hits, I blend in the crowd until they reach the library, which is where I slip away to hide out in my favorite corner, praying I won't have to face Gianna again until theater.

Opening my math book, I'm surprised when the one face I thought I had succeeded in avoiding slides into the seat across from me with a dissatisfied disposition.

"Do you remember my name?" She drops her bag beside her on the floor.

Confused by the question I slowly answer, "I do."

"So we've met before?"

Now understanding where this path of sarcasm is headed, I shut my math book, "Once or twice. You enjoying your day?"

Nonchalantly she shrugs, "Not really."

"Oh?"

"Yeah craziest thing happened. I woke up in the bed of the most amazing guy I've ever dated, next to his precious daughter," the word causes me to glare hoping she keeps her voice down. "We had breakfast and when we went separate ways to class this morning, I was under the impression everything was fine. That we were fine. Then I find him here. Avoiding me."

"What? No I'm not." I shake my head, my first lie to her being a blunt and dumb one.

"Liar."

"I like actor personally," my humor keeps me from completely digging myself into a hole.

Gianna folds her arms. "You don't want to talk to me do you?"

I don't answer, knowing I don't want to lie again.

"Why? Because I wanna talk about—"

"Sh," I hush her opening my book back up. "There are very few people who know and I work damn hard to keep it that way. Please, don't ruin it."

With a nod she leans forward on her arms, "Can we at least talk about it now?"

"Sure," my eyes don't leave the textbook that looks like nothing more than blurry random letters and numbers no matter how hard I try to concentrate. "What do you wanna know?"

"Everything," the expected answer rushes from her mouth.

"Be more specific," I mutter.

Shutting my book for me she grunts, "Can you at least look at me while you talk to me?"

Leaning back in the chair of the back corner table, I toss a hand in the air. "Fine." "How old is she?"

"2 ½. Almost three."

"So you had her when you were…"

"A little before my 16th birthday. While my friends were getting cars, I got a lifetime responsibility of a different variety."

"You sound like you were thrilled about it."

"Ecstatic," my sarcasm takes her by surprise.

"You mean to tell me you don't love—"

"No. I do love her and wouldn't trade having her for anything in the world. Make no mistake, every morning that little girl is breathing, is the happiest day of my life and I am most thankful for it. But when you're sixteen..." My head shakes slowly. "When you're sixteen, it's not only the most difficult concept to wrap your head around, but the most crucial. Someone else's life was about to be my responsibility and all I wanted to do was take back the choice that got me in the situation."

"I guess that's not hard to understand." Gianna tugs on the sleeves of her shirt, adjusts her body so she's sitting on her leg, and leans closer. "But how… how did you end up with a kid? I mean you read about stuff like this and see it on T.V., but how did you get her? I mean didn't you use a condom?"

"Yeah, but condoms are only a certain percent effective."

"Yeah, but wasn't she on the pill?"

"Ha," my laugh causes her to stir in her seat. "The pill? Could you imagine telling your mother you want to start sleeping around at 15?"

Gianna shrugs. "Not that crazy where I come from."

"Okay." I clear my throat. "Not everyone's parents feel that way. Hers definitely wouldn't have been understanding at all. Probably would've shipped her away to a convent. Hell, I wish they would have. Might have prevented their daughter from becoming the school slut."

Gianna glances away and whispers, "We have our reasons..."

My hand reaches out and turns her face back to mine. "You did. She had lies. There's a difference."

Her face softens and shoulders relax. "So, she was sleeping around. Then how do you know she's really yours?"

"DNA."

"You got a DNA test?"

"Hell yeah. There's no way I'd spend my entire life taking care of another man's child if I wasn't in love with the person."

"You weren't in love with her?'

Pressing my lips together I take a minute to push through the lingering pain and regret. "No."

"Really?"

"Really." Running my fingers through my hair I sigh, "At the time I thought I was. I wasn't in a good place in life and my bullshit radar was broken. She gave me a sob story, I later learned was what she did to the guys she wanted to keep for longer than a night. She'd weave a pity tale for you to believe, fuck you until she grew tired of you, and leave. I was the idiot who thought he loved her and that she loved him. That she had changed for me. That she'd be there for me through the shit I was going through. But I was wrong. Sometimes at night, I'll look back on it as I stroke my Mak to sleep and realize it was never love at all. Just infatuation gone terribly wrong. One horny teen dealing with the death of his father, burying his dick in something to make himself forget about it."

"Your dad--"

"Was the best man in the entire world. Loved my mom enough to leave Hawaii. His home. The only world he ever knew because there wasn't a damn thing he wouldn't do for her."

"And he...he passed away from what?"

Hating this conversation, I do my best to muscle through it. She shared her past and opened herself up to me. I should be willing to do the same if this is gonna work. And I want this to work. I feel like it needs to.

"Cancer. The nasty kind."

"Aren't they all nasty?"

"The kind that eats you alive and doesn't come up for air. I watched my father die. I watched my hero fall from the grace of heaven to the pit of a grave. It broke me and destroyed my mother."

"That's why she is..." Gianna's hand waves in the air. "The way she is with you."

"Yeah." Desperate for the conversation to end I open my text book back up. "Are we done?"

Quickly Gianna shuts the book again before using that hand to lift my chin up. "Good try, but no. Where is Mak's mother now?"

My shoulders shrug as I toy with the pages to the textbook in front of me. "Not a clue. She gave birth to MaKayla Ashley Owens and a month later skipped town while I had her one day. She left me just barely enough to get started, and I haven't heard from her since. Luckily for me I had been doing little jobs while her mother was pregnant, so I had some money saved, which was good because without it, I'm not sure that little girl would have lived."

"Wait. What?" Gianna's voice raises so loudly a girl typing on one of the computers nearby looks over. I give her a stern look and she scoots her chair to sit next to me. In a hush voice she naps, "What! What exactly happened?"

Frustrated by the memory, I stare down at the book, hoping to find a focal point that makes this conversation easier for me. "She brought her over. It was a Tuesday. I'd just quit the basketball team at school, my old school, and she said she was bringing her over to hang out with me while she went to get her haircut. She had brought me her car seat, in case I wanted to take her anywhere. All the diapers she had because she claimed she didn't think I had any and wanted me to be prepared for overnights. She brought me formula because I didn't have any. I assumed all this was just a mother being over paranoid, not like I could ask my mother about it since she had been doing her disappearing drug act. When she handed me the diaper bag, I didn't stop to check it. If I had I would've noticed it contained every piece of clothing MaKayla owned. I took all the stuff dropped it in my bedroom at the apartment and kissed her goodbye. Later that night, probably about nine after I assumed all the places to get your haircut were closed, I called her house to come to find out she never made it home. For days I waited and waited for a call to hear she was coming back, to hear she was okay, to hear she still wanted our baby girl and I never heard anything. A couple months later her mother called me to let me know that she had sent her a message to let her know she was okay, but wouldn't be coming home. Ever."

"Oh my god…" her mouth softly mumbles. "They didn't track her down?"

"I assumed they tried, but it didn't matter with her. She was definitely the kind of girl who knew what to say and how to act to get whatever it is she wanted exactly when she wanted it."

Gianna's finger softly touches the back of my hand. I don't look up. "Did she say why?"

"Why what?"

"Why she left."

"No."

She mumbles something that sounds like bitch and my face twitches a smirk at her comment. Her subtle way of expressing she hates what I went through lifts my attention up to her.

"So then what did you do? After...she ran away like a damn coward."

"The only thing I could. I got jobs when I could off the books to scrape up cash. Starved so she could eat. Switched schools to stop myself from doing more disruptive shit. When I got here, the school counselors were all desperate to help, impressed I was a single father who stayed in school and away from drugs. They arranged to cut me some leeway on tardies and helped me get a job working at the preschool almost immediately. The preschool gives me a major discount because of my situation, they can write part of it off as a charity donation thing, and then the fact I work there gets me another huge discount. All the money I make goes towards taking care of Mak, putting groceries in the house, and basically just trying to survive while my mother's money contributes mostly to paying rent, occasionally electricity and water. Now can we talk about something else? Anything else?"

"Sure," her smirk let's me know she's not giving up that easy. "How about college? Are you going?"

On a heavy exhale I shrug. "That's the hope. I've got financial aid lined up. The preschool helped cover a couple costs and have it arranged for me to work full time all summer. I got accepted to the University of Wardington right here in the city. Don't have to pay for a dorm. My shitty car can make it most days and classes all arranged for when Mak is in school. Only thing is, I need all the help I can get, which is why that scholarship is so important to me and why...you, *at* first, were a problem. I can't afford for anything to ruin my chances at college. I'm not just going to better myself, but to make my father and daughter proud. Show him, that I can be that man he expected me to, even if I faltered for a while and to show her nothing can keep you down unless you let it."

To my surprise, Gianna leans over, and slips her lips on mine. At first I barely kiss back, but when her hand touches the side of my neck, I cave like always, my inability to resist the girl worse than it was with Mak's mother. A huge problem.

She pulls away and whispers against my lips, "You are amazing you know that?"

"I do," the answer gets her to smile widely. "But so are you."

With another brief kiss, she leans back in her seat. "You ever wish she would come back?"

"Nope. Couldn't be happier she vanished. She left me with the most beautiful, sweetest, amazing child in the entire world, and if she would've stuck around no telling how she might've ended up."

"So Mak is the reason you don't come over and have been 'busy' every weekend?"

"Yeah. Gianna, I would love to take you on dates. To go to the movies or to dinner, all the things a boyfriend should do, but I can't. It's only me for Mak and she'll always come first. With money. With time. With everything. I love my little girl."

"She has no one to watch her?"

"I don't allow my mom to watch her if I'm not home. One of the admins at the preschool has watched her for a couple hours in certain situations like for a school performance, but other than that no. No babysitters. She's never met any of my friends even though Bret and Brent both know she exists. You are the first person I've brought around her like that."

"It wasn't by choice," Gianna reminds me with a sharp look. "And something tells me if the situation wouldn't have happened, you would've continued to keep her as a secret from me. My question is for how long?"

The intensity from her stare pushes my eyes away to the digital clock on the wall.

"Connor."

I press my lips together to remain silent. These last two days have been a fucking nightmare and they don't need to get worse. They just...don't.

"Connor."

"Forever," I snap finally looking her back in the eyes. "Forever Gianna. I would've kept Mak hidden until you grew bored of me or we had some fight that inevitably pulled us apart. I would've kept her separate from this situation as long as possible."

In a hurt whisper she questions, "Because you don't trust me?"

"Because I don't trust myself." The confession floors her jaw. "Look at my life Gianna. I don't make great choices. I have bruises on my body because I can't help myself from taking the hits so my mother doesn't have to. I live in a run-down shitty apartment instead of a beach in Hawaii because I can't abandon the woman my father loved more than his own life. I have a toddler to take care of because fucking away my problems was the only solution I could come up with. I don't trust myself to do anything right, so instead of complicating the choices I'm already always facing with you...you and all the mixed up feelings that come along with you, keeping you at a distance was the plan."

"Plans don't always work."

"Trust me," I say bitterly. "I know."

"So now what?" Gianna folds her arms across her chest. "You're gonna dump me because I know your dirty little secret?"

"Don't refer to her that way."

"Why not?" She shrugs. "That's how you're treating it."

"Please don't judge me." I shake my head. "That's one of the reasons I don't want people to know. I don't need the judgment. I don't need pity masked as kindness. I have enough of that bullshit already."

Seeing her back down, rearranges a little room to breathe. "So was that it? Are you gonna break up with me because I know? That's not fair. You know my secrets and have helped me. Now I know yours and can help you."

Bitterly I reiterate, "We. Are. Not. A. Charity. Case."

"I didn't say you were," she squeaks loudly, the girl on the computer turning to look at us again. This time Gianna shoots her a dirty look until she looks away. "What I'm saying is, let me be the one that tries to understand you and what you're going through. You shouldn't have to be in this alone. Let's take Mak to do things on my dime."

"Gi--"

"Sh. I *want* to do this. I *want* to be around her. There's nothing more I wanna do than spend time with the guy I'm dating and if that includes the cutest kid in the world, well then that's what we do. And it's not like I'm hurting for money Connor. And it's not like I need any more crap. I've got enough clothes and shoes and pointless shit I don't use to last me a life time. It would be so much more fun to spend it on someone who would appreciate it. Who appreciates life in a way I should. I just wanna be around you and Mak even if that means we're just going to the park and swinging. Time with you is time with you no matter where that is."

A slight smile creeps on my face as the anxiety starts to shift. "You really want to try to make something work huh?"

"More than you know," she whispers. "I've never met a guy like you and I'm not ready to give you up yet."

My fingers slide over to fold with hers like some driving force I can't see is linking us together in this moment. I whisper back, "I'm not ready to give you up either."

Something I am loving more than her fantastic legs pops up. Her smile. Leaning her lips towards mine she whispers one more thing, "Then don't."

Once more our lips are together and tongues tangling to start a conversation they are both more comfortable having. I don't know what the fuck I'm doing any more, but I'm just glad I don't have to do it alone. I'm so Goddamn tired of being alone.

Chapter 11

    For the next couple of weeks my entire life is flipped upside down. During school hours, when Gianna and I aren't making out, we're working on our scene to secure us that win. She gets up early, crosses town to have breakfast with Mak and I before taking her to school, and then us. Gianna's done things like go grocery shopping with us, making sure to grab healthy things and fun things she thinks kids should enjoy. Mak always leaves the store with a new book or toy. I wanna fuss at her, tell her it's too much every time, but after having the same fight four nights in a row, I stopped wasting my breath. Gianna's going to do what she wants to do and it drives me fucking crazy, but I love her for it. And I understand her, after all, I'm the same way. She's helps me clean up the house and watch Mak while I fix things that are falling apart and replace the locks. At first Mom was pissed about the new addition to the family and the changing of the locks, but she's growing into the perks of both. We've done a couple more sleepovers, but only on the weekends. While she typically leaves an hour or so after Mak goes to bed, we spend that hour getting closer and closer to that line I'm not ready to cross quite yet. Thankfully she understands and has been enjoying the perks of my hands that she says can fix more than just doors. Let's just say her hands can do more than handle make up brushes.

    The Friday on the tail end of Spring Break, which was filled with early morning trips to the local zoo, the aquarium, the park, and lunch dates before Mak and I would arrive at the school for the afternoon, she buys three tickets for us to go to the beach, claiming she misses it but doesn't wanna visit it alone. I'm almost certain she just thinks of it as a trip, but the choice of location claws at something in the back of my mind. I haven't been to the beach since my father died. It was his sanctuary. A place he always felt at home and connected to something bigger than himself. There's a fear that returning to his sacred place, I'll have to face the disappointment I know would be lingering if he were still alive. Then again, if he were still alive, many of the choices I made, I wouldn't have.

    I would've continued to fight against the idea of the trip except it's MaKayla's birthday weekend and the anxiety of not knowing the next time we'll get something this magical gets the better of me.

"You okay?" Gianna grabs my attention from the trail of thoughts mainly littered with self-doubt.

Before I have a chance to respond, MaKayla who's coloring in one of her brand new coloring books that Gianna bought her, holds up the picture of a princess and prince. "Look! It's so pretty!"

"It is! Is that you?"

"No," Mak giggles her small feet kicking her own seat in her brand new white flip flops that reveal her painted toes. "It's you and Daddy."

"Of course it is," I comment. "I'm always yellow."

She snickers and playfully elbows me before asking my daughter, "Want something to eat?"

Returning her attention to her picture she replies, "No thank you..."

"Are you okay?" Gianna turns the question to me.

"I'm good." I smile back. "Why are you so worried?"

"I remember the first time I flew how nervous I was. I just want to make sure you're okay."

"I am. I've flown before, it's just...it's been awhile."

With a deep exhale she relaxes into her seat and folds her fingers with mine. I smile softly at her before giving my daughter another glance. In a white dress with polka dots, she keeps calling her birthday dress, I whisper to Gianna, "You know, you do way too much for us."

"I don't wanna fight," she insists looking away.

"I'm not trying to fight." When she turns her body back to mine, I lift her hand to my lips for a quick kiss. "I'm just trying to make sure you know that that's not why I wanna be with you. I mean, all the clothes you bought Mak and the few you've bought me--"

"Speaking of, please tell me you brought those baby blue and white plaid shorts I love so much."

Ignoring her outburst I continue, "Not to mention the toys, the groceries, the in-town adventures and now this trip. I'm thankful for all of it, for every moment, but if you couldn't do this for us, or with us, I'd still be there with you, making this work."

In a teasing smile she giggles, "Yeah? It's cause I'm hot right?"

Seeing she's in no mood to hear my praise of gratitude, I roll my eyes.

Playfully she says, "Oh no. Daddy's making his grumpy face. What should we do Mak?"

"Tickle him!" she squeals clapping her hands before watching to see if Gianna goes through with it.

As soon as she tries, I grab her hands and reverse the tickles, filling our section of the plane with laughter. We wrestle from our buckled in seats, while Mak returns to coloring. Eventually the tickles turn into gentle touches, which lead to a heated kiss we try to stay away from when my daughter is around. Fuck me. I'm not sure how much longer I can keep putting myself in the position to have to dip my nuts in ice in an attempt cool the hell down.

A couple hours later, we're settled in our top level hotel room after a nice lunch at a kid friendly restaurant directly on the beach. The three of us change into our swimsuits before heading down to the beach we can see from our hotel.

I take Mak into the water while Gianna sets up an area for us to report back to when we're done. The two of us slowly head towards the water I know is going to be freezing, anxious for two completely different reasons.

"Daddy," Mak squeaks. "Hold me!"

"Nope," I reply. "You're gonna let the water and sand touch your feet."

"Daddy," she whines. "What if it bites me?"

With a smirk, I look down at her and remember what my father told me when I was afraid of the same thing, "The water doesn't bite Mak."

Our feet finally reach the cold water and she giggles, "It's cold..."

A smile spreads across my face as her laughter gets louder, soon followed by the urge to start splashing around, welcoming the water, the way I was hoping. The way my father would be proud of her. We move around together, her picking up seashells at the sight of them, riding on my back as we go a little deeper, and jumping on small waves together. Occasionally I look behind us seeing Gianna take pictures of us with her Nikon camera and her phone. Her own hatred of social media soothed my worries she would post all our time together blasting the personal life I wanna keep personal. However, she hasn't posted even a single photo of us as a couple, declaring she has nothing to prove with a picture. She takes so many of everything I've started to wonder if maybe being behind the camera is her true calling.

Once we're both soaking wet and Mak is exhausted with a bucket of seashells, we head for Gianna, who's set up an area for my princess to rest with a snack waiting and me a chair to relax in beside her.

"Mommy! Mommy!" Mak calls to Gianna at the top of her lungs crawling down me to rush to her lap.

Immediately the two of us lock eyes. After a moment she opens her mouth, preparation to correct her swimming in her eyes, when I clear my throat to grab her attention. The moment she looks at me again, I shake my head in a clear indication to let it go. I should probably have this conversation with Mak right now. Correct it. Put it in perspective as best as possible to a three year old, but there's a gnawing inside me that just can't. It's feels like someone has clamped their fingers on my tongue insisting to let this pass. Not to take away the hope of a child. The faith that life can give you good things. Ha. It's almost as if my father is trying to help even now. A finger unconsciously runs across my tattoo at the same time I offer Gianna a smile to relax.

"Yeah?" Gianna answers as Mak's tiny wet body bounces up and down in her lap.

"The water is so pretty!"

Warmly she smiles at her, "Is it?"

"Yeah! I found seashells! Look!" Without waiting for any sort of response she keeps talking, "I saw fish too!"

"Good birthday then?"

"BEST birthday!"

"Good! That's what I wanna hear. I'm glad you had fun with your daddy!"

"You come when we go back!"

"Yes," Gianna answers. "I didn't go this time because I wanted to take pictures."

"Can I see?"

"In a little while. Why don't you go have a snack on your towel and pick out your favorite shells for us to make a necklace out of?"

"Okay!" She squeaks and kisses Gianna on the lips before sliding off of her.

Leaning over I slyly say, "Since you're given out kisses..."

"Uh-huh," her remark is accompanied with a smile. Sweetly she lifts her lips up to mine, planting a hand on my cheek.

I part my lips just briefly to tease her tongue before pulling back to whisper, "I hope that didn't freak you out. What she called you."

In a whisper back she says, "It felt perfect." I open my mouth to say something and she cuts me off. "Just like being with you."

Unprompted Mak calls out, "I love you Daddy!"

Glancing to the side, I see my daughter with a juice box in one hand and a pile of seashells beside her.

"I love you Mak!" I yell back before settling my eyes back into my girlfriend's, "And I love you too Gianna."

Without hesitation she says, "I love you too."

My heart swells so fast and painfully full, I feel it could burst in my chest. I peck her lips once more before settling in the lounge seat beside her. As I cover my eyes, I look out at the beautiful blue water that the sunlight is quickly heating, just like love in my entire world. Looking out at the sight feels like I'm looking into my father's blue eyes, the peacefulness of it all, approval that I've finally found myself again.

Chapter 12

About a week and half after our vacation together, life is still smooth sailing, so smooth in fact, I know I should be waiting for the other shoe to drop, for some hiccup like a sick daughter who I have to miss school for or a test I forgot to study for. I've been trying to focus all my energy on just enjoying every minute that falls in my lap with the two girls who together have given me back the life I thought I'd never see again.

"So everything with the therapist is still going good?" I munch down on my banana enjoying our Wednesday lunch alone.

"Yeah." Gianna grabs a grape off my plate. "She's impressed with my progress. She definitely thinks being around you and Mak have been great for my perspective in regards to food. We're working heavily on changing my negative view of it and also focusing on other aspects of my life to shift the attention to something more productive."

"Well don't you sound like a grown up."

The joke makes her swat a hand at me from across the table before taking a chip out the bag beside me. "Oh shut up." After a beat she sighs, "So I've been thinking..."

"Is this about sex?" I toss the peel to the side. "Because we just talked about it."

Shaking her head she denies, "No. No. Not that. Though I will say while I am looking forward to that even more if what you can do with your hands and tongue are any kind of prelude to what's to come."

Pride forces my body to sit up straight. "I like to think they are an understatement in comparison to what's to come."

A tiny whimper comes from Gianna. Quickly she shakes her head again. "Anyway, I've been thinking...I want you to come over for dinner to meet my parents."

"I don't think that's a good idea," I declare. "At all."

"Oh come on. My parents would love to meet you."

"I highly doubt that."

"Why?"

"Because I don't...we aren't..." the words get tangled and frustration causes me to drop a heavy sigh. "I just don't think it's a good idea."

"And I didn't think you taking surf lessons was a good idea, but I let you."

"What? Why? I told you I grew up around the water..."

"Years ago," she emphasizes. "But I trusted your judgment. Now trust mine. Come on Connor, I rarely ask you for much...can you do this for me please? It would mean a lot."

Guilt starts sinking to the pit of my stomach. She's right. In this relationship she's asked for very little. Not that I've asked for much either, but she's giving more and more of her life, herself to us, every day. Sure. We are too, but she's giving financial support as well as emotional. The least I can do is give her extra emotional crap when she asks for it, no matter if I agree with it or not.

In a low grumble I surrender. "Fine."

"Really?" the excitement stomps my own unhappiness further down.

"Really, but not too late. You know what Mak's like when she's up too late."

"Grouchy." She raises her water bottle. Before having a sip she giggles, "Apple didn't fall far from the tree there."

I shoot her a glare and she snickers. "You're lucky I love you."

"That I am," her reply warms my face, the final killer to any crabbiness from the situation that is probably not going to be anywhere as painful as I'm imagining.

Around 7:40 the two of us are driving through Gianna's mansion gates in my car that runs better than it has in the entire time I've owned it. While we went out of town for vacation, we left my car behind and Gianna had someone take it and fix everything they could, making it the closest thing to a brand new car it could be, without actually having to buy a new one. The only reason she didn't get me a new car was because I refused. I already owe her a kidney at this rate. Couldn't afford to have to owe her my right nut too.

In the back MaKayla kicks her feet in excitement. "Daddy! Daddy! Look at the castle! Is that mommy's castle?"

"It sure is."

"It's so big! Can we live in it too Daddy? Mommy has lots of room for us. I just know it."

I sigh, "Someday we will live in our own castle Mak."

"With Mommy? Like a new castle? I would love a new castle!"

My lips press together uncomfortably at the line of questioning. I know she's just being a three year old, but the questions are ones that have been keeping me up at night since we got back from our vacation. Where the hell is this gonna end? Moving in together? Marriage? More kids? These aren't questions I should have to ask, but they are. Fuck me they really are.

Not surprised at the sight of Gianna waiting for us outside, I point, "Look Mak. There she is."

"Mommy!" She claps and waves. "Does she see us! She sees us! Hi mommy!"

The repetition of the name has me wanting to sit down with Gianna and talk about the direction we're heading. I know we've glazed over it once or twice, touched on it occasionally, but if we're going to keep behaving like a family, I owe it to Mak to make sure that's where we're headed 100%. And if it is, I will definitely welcome it.

After I park, I get out, adjust my button down white shirt and smile. "Good evening Gianna."

"Good evening Connor," she says in a snooty seductive voice, the silliness clear to both of us. After a quick kiss she compliments, "You look fantastic."

"So do you..." I admire her black tube top cocktail dress that is displaying a few extra healthy curves on her body, but more importantly is highlighting one, her legs. Legs that I know will look even sexier over my shoulders. Damn. Once we have this talk, we're definitely having sex. As if she heard me, she kisses me again, this time rolling her tongue around in my mouth just tempting enough to make me groan in sexual aggravation. Pulling away, I sigh, "Really? You want me to walk in to meet your parents like this?"

She giggles before opening Mak's door, "Well hello there Princess!"

"Mommy!" Mak squeals and reaches out for her to hold her.

Gianna undoes her car seat, pulls her into her arms. "Your dress looks very pretty."

"It's my Cinderella dress!" She smiles and wiggles around in her puffy white dress she insisted on having.

"It's so beautiful I think Cinderella would be jealous of you," Gianna says.

"Of me?" Mak's jaw hits the ground.

"Yup. You are the prettiest princess I've ever seen." After my daughter giggles again, Gianna asks, "Who bought your dress?"

"Daddy did," Mak answers twirling her finger around one of the ringlets in Gianna's pinned up hair. "We left school early today."

"You bought her a dress to wear for tonight?" Gianna looks touched.

Trying not to blush I nod. "Yeah. I know this night means a lot to you, so I figure a little splurge wouldn't hurt. Nelly let me off an hour early as long as I promised to make it up."

"Aw." She coos as I slide my arm around her waist walking towards her front door with her. "You didn't have to do that Connor. Seriously."

"I didn't any more than you have to do what you do for us." Her face twitches a smirk. "I guess it's what people do in love."

We enter the mansion and immediately Mak starts squealing and talking about how excited she is to finally be in a princesses' castle. At the speed Mak is talking, I miss at least half of what she says, but catch the gist of it, the most important being when are we all living in a castle together.

"Mak, we'll talk about all that someday," I assure her. "Just not today okay?"

"We will?" Gianna's eyebrows rise.

"Unless you don't want to."

"No I do!" She rushes out.

"Me too..."

Excited she leans over to kiss me when Mak's hands grabs her face giving me a new reference for cock block. "Can we have a puppy in our castle?"

"No more castle questions tonight." I firmly say.

"But Daddy--"

"MaKayla Ashley."

She pouts with a grumpy face and looks at Gianna for sympathy.

"Oh no you don't." Gianna shakes her head. "I'm with your daddy on this one. No more castle talk. Did I tell you we're having ice cream tonight?"

"Ice cream!" Mak squeaks.

The three of us stroll into the formal dining room, which is what I picture the back room of a five star restaurant to be like, from the white table cloths, to the seating, wine glasses, and stale but ritzy feeling.

"Where are your parents?" I ask nervously sticking my hands in my dress pants pockets. The only pair of dress pants I own. Didn't feel the need for them when Gianna assured me they would come in handy. I figured maybe for a job interview not for a relationship one.

"Upstairs," she sighs adjusting MaKayla on her hip. "Arguing."

"About?

"Who cares," her answer should've been predicted. They barely acknowledge their daughter exists any more. Not once has she mentioned them complaining she doesn't come home or about her sneaking out before school starts. According to her they are just thankful she's keeping their name clean this time. "Probably nothing important. You know, why Dad spent the night downtown on his 'day off' or why Mom spent 400 dollars on brunch if she went by herself. Heaven forbid they argue about why their daughter decided she wanted to go to college in the city instead of out of state or how I decided that photography would be a better career path for me than being a doctor."

"You wanted to be a doctor?"

"Never," she answers quickly. "But they thought it would be a good idea if I took classes that direction and eventually met the right people. My father lives by many rules, but the golden one is, always ask 'What can this person do for me'?"

"That seems...cynical. Manipulative."

"You don't make millions by asking how they take their tea," her snide remark churns my stomach.

Footsteps suddenly approach, which causes us to turn around to see a butler entering the room.

"Good evening, my name is John, and I'll be taking care of you this evening. Can I get you a drink while you wait to be seated for dinner?" He asks as if we were in an actual restaurant.

"Yes please. Just a water for me and some sort of juice for her." I casually point to Mak who is playing with the necklace around Gianna's neck.

Politely he questions in return. "Of course sir. What sort of juice would you like?"

"What do you have?"

"Apple, orange, cranberry, pineapple, and grape. We also have a variety of those that can be freshly made from scratch if you would prefer."

"Apple please," Mak squeals as Gianna bats at her little hands to make her giggle.

"And a booster chair please," Gianna instructs kissing her cheek at the same time my daughter begs to explore the castle.

"And what would you like to drink Ms. Gianna?"

"Waters fine for me as well," she answers letting Mak slide down her body. Still holding onto her hand. "Come on you two. I'll give you the tour."

Mak wiggles her fingers at me. "Come on Daddy! I wanna see if she has a dragon!"

Grabbing my daughter's free hand I sigh, "I doubt she has a dragon."

With a sneaky smirk Gianna says, "But you don't really know do you..."

I roll my eyes as the three of us wander off to see the place she rarely ever calls home.

We're gone longer than expected between Mak's million questions and Gianna's desire to make out with me around corners and doors while Mak toyed with random objects to go along with songs she sang from various princess movies. Finally returning to the dining room, we see her parents standing with beverages in their hands. Her father a martini glass. Her mother an almost empty wine glass.

"There you are," the woman who has obviously given Gianna her looks and body structure, sighs trying to smile. "We were beginning to think you changed your mind."

"I was just showing them around to pass the time while you and Dad finished your discussion." In a swift motion she picks up my little girl. "Mom and Dad, this is MaKayla and Connor Owens."

"Cecile." Her mother extends a delicate hand at me. She's only a size bigger than Gianna, with a short bobbed haircut, and a painted face to give a flaw free image that my girlfriend used to. Lately, she goes for an almost natural look unless we're going out to dinner and even then, it's just enough for her to feel comfortable. She's so beautiful without all the added crap on her face. However, looking at her mother now and knowing the model lifestyle she used to lead, it's no wonder why it's taking her so long to realize it. Someday she's gonna have to tell Mak about this girly shit. I just hope that she remembers that she's more beautiful without it and let's that be her guide in transitioning my daughter into that. Fuck. I'm not ready for that. No fucking way. Good thing that's light-years away. Eons.

"Pleasure," I politely shake.

Less impressed by my presence is her 6'4, dark as midnight skinned, bald headed father. He holds out his large palm, "Donald."

Firmly I shake, "Sir."

"My name is MaKayla!" my daughter enters the conversation. "You have a castle! It's so big! It's bigger than all the ones in my movies and my coloring books. You're missing a dragon..."

Gianna's mother slyly says, "He sleeps under the house."

"I knew it!" MaKayla looks at me immediately after. "I told you daddy..."

My girlfriend adds as she slides Mak into her booster seat at the table, "I tried to tell him too."

Shaking my head with a smile at the playful nature I prepare to pull Gianna's chair out for her when she insists, "You don't have to Baby. John does that."

In a mutter her father says, "He behaves like the help. Anyone surprised?"

"Donald," his wife hisses sitting at the opposite end of the table from him, where a maid is pulling out her chair.

I push down the bewilderment of the snide remark and sit down beside my daughter whose attention is all over the place. Thankfully John places a glass of juice in a child friendly cup, a coloring book, and crayons in front of her.

"Thank you!" She squeaks loudly.

"Thank you," I say directly after her.

"You both have such wonderful manners," Cecile compliments as her glass of wine is refilled.

"Thank you," my face shoots her a smile even though I'm sure her husband mumbles something distasteful. It's already painful enough having to meet your girlfriend's parents without them judging you for breathing incorrectly, but I have a feeling that Donald's behavior is only going to get worse.

A menu is placed in front of me and a baffled look pops on my face as my eyes meet Gianna's. She tries to give me a look to indicate it's alright. I find that hard to believe. Who the hell has menus at *home* for dinner time?

"You're welcomed to anything on the menu." Her mother gestures lifting her own menu.

I glance down at the piece of paper at the same time Gianna adds, "Feel free to order anything even if it's not on the menu. They can make hamburgers, hot dogs, hot pockets, whatever. Just whatever you and MaKayla would like."

"Chicken nuggets!" Mak declares.

Quickly I deny, "You may not have chicken nuggets."

"But Daddy—"

"No buts." I shake my head slowly.

"But--"

Gianna takes my side. "Mak, we had chicken nuggets for dinner two nights ago. No chicken nuggets."

"You had chicken nuggets?' Her mother scoffs. "Do you have any idea the unnatural ingredients in those?"

"I do," she responds sharply. "And I did, except they weren't frozen or pre bought. We got chicken, coated it, and baked it ourselves."

"We?" Donald looks at her with a cold look.

"Connor and I," Gianna says strongly. "We make dinner at his place quite often. Well balanced meals and more importantly a variety of things for Mak to grow accustomed too." Suddenly she turns her attention to me, "Remember when she tried asparagus?"

I lightly chuckle, "Yeah. Green Fingers."

"I love green fingers," Mak mutters to no one in particular. "Can I have Green Fingers tonight?"

"You sure can," Gianna answers for me.

"I think that's a great idea," I agree reaching for a blue crayon to color with her.

"So that's where you've been most nights for dinner?" Donald sits back in his seat.

"You would both know that if you listened when I talked," she snaps.

"Let's not fight," Cecile insists handing her menu to John. "I'll have my usual. Nothing is standing out tonight."

He nods and approaches us, "And for the two of you?"

"Um..." I glance at the menu filled with things that are as expensive as everything else in the house. Wanting to impress Gianna is pushing me out of my comfort zone. I don't belong here. We shouldn't be here. For food much less for conversation. This is all wrong. This feels wrong.

"I'll have a bacon cheeseburger," Gianna's voice catches my attention. My eyes rise to hers to see her smiling, giving me her clear vote of confidence. She's on my side. Even through this shit. She's still on my side. "With sweat potato fries. Fresh pineapple chunks please."

Taking the clue, I turn to John, "I'll have that too. And for Mak she'll have a kid's size cheeseburger, with asparagus and strawberries."

"Daddy can I have fries please?" Her small voice pleads.

"I'll share mine." I kiss the side of her face. "Why don't you color her hair red?"

"Daddy I know what I'm doing," she giggles focusing back on her picture.

John nods before walking over to Donald who orders a steak rare. The bloodier the better I bet. For once I shouldn't be surprised. Unlike him I try to see around what's in front of me. Gianna's taught me that much. Well, we've taught each other that.

After John and the maid whose name I don't know excuse themselves, Cecile speaks up, "So tell us a little about yourself Connor. Like for instance, how did you and our beautiful daughter meet?"

"We were assigned partners in our theater class," I reply making sure to give her eye contact, all the etiquette rules my mother used to try to instill in me when I was younger finally coming in handy.

"You're still in that useless thing?" Donald rolls his eyes.

"Yes," Gianna groans.

"We spoke about this."

"We did. And since it's clear you do not recall I will refresh your memory. I enjoy the exploration of the arts, which includes theater. Being given a creative outlet has done wonders for the rest of my grades, if you noticed, plus Dr. Jean believes having a healthy place to focus my anxiety is necessary."

"You shouldn't be seeing her. There's nothing wrong with you," he insists.

"Clearly..." She mumbles back.

Doing her best to try to redirect the conversation, her mother clears her throat and speaks loudly, "So you're partners?"

I do my best to drag my attention away from them. I don't understand how he can treat her that way. He has one daughter. One child. One life to nurture and love and he doesn't. I'll never treat Mak that way. Sure, every choice she makes won't be the best, but who am I to judge when I got her before I got my license. More importantly, you should be building your only offspring up, not tearing them down.

Cecile's voice speaks again, "Connor?"

"Sorry ma'am." I clear my throat. "Yes, we are. It's funny. We didn't really get along at first, but we grew to find we have a lot more in common than we thought."

"I doubt that," her father snips. "Tell me. Why are you in such a useless class?"

"I aspire to be an actor someday," I answer. "At the very least something in that field feels like a calling to me. Maybe a director. Maybe a producer. Whatever it is, I know it's in that world. Who knows, maybe I'll learn to cut trailers."

"He's really good though." Gianna gushes. "He's played leads in the majority of the plays and those he wasn't he played the understudy lead and the supporting actor. On top of acting he can sing and dance. The star of the school musical this year and got them in the local paper."

Cecile coos in a genuine tone, "Impressive."

I nod, "Thank you."

"They're expecting our scene to win at this year's scholarship festival."

"And I'm sure we will. We make a good team." I wink at her, which makes her giggle in her seat, something that makes her mother excited and her father annoyed.

"So is that why you're into my daughter? Because you know I've got connections to the acting world?" her father bites. "Sleep your way up the ladder? Is that your angle?"

"Donald stop," Cecile hisses.

Instinctively I assure him, "We're not sleeping together."

"We sleep together all the time!" Mak looks up confused.

"That's right Mak," Gianna tries to calm her down. "We all sleep in the same bed sometimes." Looking at her father she growls, "I agree with Mom. Stop it."

"So you two didn't get along? What changed?" Cecile asks as a salad is presented to her.

"We actually stopped and gave each other a chance," I answer with a short chuckle. "We're both a little introverted—"

"Hot tempered," Gianna slides it in.

"Stubborn," we say in unison, which is followed by a snicker from both of us.

"Cute," her mother mutters.

"Irritating." Donald disagrees.

For the next twenty minutes, give or take, I'm interrogated by her father, redirected by her mother, and the fuel behind every snide remark Gianna makes to them. The tension is not ideal for me, damn sure not for my daughter, but I'm thankful Mak spends most of her time coloring and talking to the pictures. Finally when the meal arrives, her father tucks his verbal sword away long enough to enjoy steak. During the meal Cecile takes this as a perfect chance to turn the topic of his job, his employees, his friends, anything that keeps me away from the spotlight.

About the time he's finished, Gianna gets up to show Mak a surprise she's been holding onto all day for her, insisting I stay to talk to her parents, which has nightmare written all over it. She's seen what they are capable of. Why leave me to fend for myself with the sharks? If they hate me with her in the room, how much more can they hate me without her in it?

The second she's out of sight her mother makes a quick attempt to pave the possible rough start. "You know she's so beautiful. She's looks just like you."

"Thank you."

"And she's just as sweet and politely mannered as you," she continues to compliment me, the alluring idea that this isn't about to end in shambles slightly more believable.

"And Gianna is, well..." Her mother pauses determining just the right way to word it. "Attached to her. Both of you actually. I don't think I've ever seen Gianna so dedicated to helping another person. This is the highest her grades have ever been. The most responsible. It's quite amazing. She's really changed so much, I almost don't recognize her."

"I know I don't." Donald clears his throat as his coffee is placed on the table. "And while we've always encouraged her to do charity work, this crosses the line."

"Donald!" His wife yells.

"Excuse me?" I raise my eyebrows, the blood rushing through my body towards my tensing neck the same way it does when I prepare to take a blow from my stepfather. "Are you implying Gianna's only interested in for a makeover? To be my source of income? To treat me like her own Ken doll on welfare? Save me like I'm sort of dude version of Cinderella?"

"Now we're on the same page." Donald shoots me a wink. I grip the edge of my chair to hold in my rage.

"I'm sorry, but with all due respect sir, I think you're wrong." I do my best to stand up for myself.

"I don't think so," Cecile nervously counters. "No offense Connor. You are a remarkable individual--"

"Don't lie to the boy—"

"Donald!" She fusses again. He shuts his mouth. "You are clearly a nice young man, but Gianna's not ready to be a mother. She's definitely not responsible enough to actually be a stepmother. I'm sure she's having fun babysitting now, wining and dining you both, but soon the high will wear off like it does with all of her pet projects, and she'll realize that this is just like when she got a pony and swore she'd take care of it night and day and eventually well—"

Disgusted, I growl, "Are you comparing my daughter to a pony?"

"Not exactly. Just the situation," Cecile tries to clarify.

Unsure of how to respond appropriately, I clench my fists tightly together, seal my lips, and nod slowly. He compared me to a charity project. She's comparing my princess to a fucking horse. This can't possibly be actually happening to me. This shit doesn't happen in real life. No. No way.

"Why don't you just admit you're using my daughter for her money hmm?" Her father slides his coffee cup back on its saucer. "How much is this going to cost me to make you go away? I mean really, single parent at eighteen who can barely take care of himself let alone his daughter just so *magically* ends up paired with the richest girl in the school, the city, if not the state, and they just so happen to end up dating even though they have nothing in common. Chances of this not being some sort of set up, maybe on your part, maybe on a pathetic teachers part, are slim. You like the money you're receiving while my daughter likes the feeling of being worth something. Like she's finally giving something back for all the shit she's managed to take. So my question to you Connor, I repeat, is how much is it going to cost me to make you and your white trash family disappear from her life?"

Suddenly, Gianna and Mak come rounding the corner, my daughter holding a brand new baby doll.

"Let's go Princess." I stand still in disbelief.

"Okay Daddy," she giggles. Looking up at Gianna she asks, "Mommy are you coming too?"

"No." My voice bites as I head towards her.

The hurt look on Gianna's face can't be missed, but she pushes through it. "So soon? You're not going to stay and—"

"No," I cut her off trying to stifle my rage. "I need to get Mak home for bed."

She tries again, "But I thought—"

"No."

"Why are you being short with me?" Gianna raises an eyebrow.

"I'm not."

"Yes you are," she deeply sighs.

"I am not."

She starts again, "Connor—"

"Let's go. And Mak, give Gianna back the doll," my instruction causes a stir from both of them.

"No," my daughter pouts. "She gave it to me. It's mine."

"And Daddy wants you to give it back," I grump arriving in front of her. "Now."

"Why?" Gianna's voice rises. "It was a gift—"

"No."

"But—"

"I said no."

"Can I finish my sentence please?" She snaps at me loudly. "What's the matter with you anyways? Since when do you cut me off all the time?"

"Look, I need to get her home, and I want her to leave the doll. We're not a charity case."

"I know that!" My eyes glance at her parents, which is where her eyes dart to, "What did you say…What did you say to him?"

"Nothing," I swallow hard. "Let's go MaKayla, tell everyone good night."

"But I wanna keep the doll daddy!" She screams at me. "It's mine!"

"No sweetie."

"Yes!"

"No."

"Yes!"

"No!"

"Yes! I want to!" She screams at the top of her lungs. Tears start to fill her eyes at a rapid rate as she flops to the ground clutching the doll for dear life. "I want it! Mommy gave it to me! It looks just like me Daddy! It's a present from Mommy…please don't make me give it back."

The sound of her tears, the phrase, and the situation cuts too deep for me to breathe. "Mak…please leave the doll."

She begins to bawl, the sight shifting tears in my own eyes to point I have to look at the ceiling to prevent them from escaping.

"Can't control his own daughter, what could he possibly bring to the table?" Her father mumbles loud enough for everyone to hear.

"You couldn't control yours either," my voice harshly snaps looking at him. Immediately he rises to his feet. "What did you say?"

"Donald. Sit down," her mother instructs.

128

Before saying something else that's out of line, I swoop up Mak, pull the doll out of her hands, shove it back at Gianna before saying coldly to her parents. "Goodnight."

With Mak crying and screaming, her tantrum making me wish I could do the same, I head out of the dining room at the same time I hear Gianna snap, "I will deal with you when I get back." Rushing to me she reaches me right as my hand hits the front door knob. "Wait! Wait!"

Between trying to leave and trying to handle Mak my level of frustration peaks, "What Gianna?"

"Look I don't know what they said to you—"

"It's not important—"

"And I'm sure it hurt your feelings—"

"It doesn't matter—"

"I just don't want what happened in there to ruin what we've got—"

"Goodnight Gianna," is the last thing I say before stepping to the other side of the door.

"Connor!" She calls at me one last time. Turning around she holds the doll out, "Please, just take the doll."

Pulling it from her hands, feels like I'm pulling our future apart at the same time. Putting back in place the independence that I once swore by. That I should still swear by, because they're right. What 18 year old girlfriend wouldn't grow weary and tired of the responsibility of being a parent when the good times stop rolling? When the pressures of financial responsibilities become overwhelming, when the time you have to cancel for things you wanna do comes because she's sick, or when you realize that you don't ever get to have a life of your very own again.

My eyes cut down to Mak as I hand her the doll. "Say goodbye MaKayla Ashley."

"Bye Mommy." She waves before resting her head on my shoulder not knowing this goodbye isn't temporary like it has been in the past. No. This is me doing the right thing. Stopping all this before it's too deep and there is no point of return. How fucking stupid was I to think this would end well with us moving in together or anything like that when we graduated? This isn't some fucking movie. There is no such thing as Happily Ever After.

Chapter 13

Barging into my apartment my daughter passed out in my arms, gripping the doll tighter than she does her favorite teddy bear, I try to ignore the pain that it's going to cause me to have to rip both Gianna and the damn doll from her world.

The minute I'm inside I'm surprised to see my mother sitting on the couch soberly with what I swear is a ghost. Trying to close the door quietly as possible while stifling my urge to yell I stare at what has to be a figment of my imagination. There's no way this shit is happening to me. No way this fucking day can get any worse without imploding.

Exhausted I growl, "What the fuck are you doing here?"

"Hey!" My mother clears her throat. "Don't be rude Connor! Go put MaKayla to bed and come back please."

My eyes dart down to a glare at my mother, "I want her out before I get back."

"Just go," my mother shoos me away.

I refuse to give either of them another look. I take MaKayla to our bedroom where I lay her down in her dress. Slowly I start to try to pull it off when she begins kicking severely, waking up out of her sleep. Thank God it wasn't a moment sooner. Not sure I can handle that in combination with the world's worst dinner.

"No Daddy." She pushes my hands away.

"What now?"

"I don't wanna take it off."

On a deep sigh I argue, "Don't you want to get in your pajamas?"

"No," she yawns clearly seconds from passing back out. "My princess dress. I wanna sleep in my princess dress. I love it. I love it so much. Please Daddy. Please."

"Fine." I surrender with a kiss to her forehead. Laying her down on her side of the bed I pull her blanket over her as she snuggles with the new doll that does look just like her right down to the bright green eyes. "You want Daddy to pat your back?"

"Yes please," she yawns again, this time her eyelids falling.

My hand pats her back while I stare down at her. I know she doesn't need the pat. She's out less than 10 pats in, but I need the moment. Just one to try to settle the emotions from dealing with Gianna's parents before having to deal with the disaster that lies on the other side of our door now. Removing my hand from Mak's back, I bury my face in it and my other one, not sure if I can force myself up to my feet. Can't this day just be fucking over already?

Relaxed enough to not try to destroy my apartment over the shit cards I'm being dealt in life, I stroll into the living room. My hands are stuffed deeply in my pockets, a stern look is on my face, and I let out a deep sigh, "What the fuck are you still doing here?"

"Can't a girl get a hello?" She shakes her head folding her arms across her chest.

"No, but a girl can get the hell out." I tilt my head towards the door.

"Connor!" my mother snaps. "You shouldn't be so rude."

"Really? This coming from the woman who has cursed her name since she walked out the door and left MaKayla with us," I state making my mother blush.

"Hush," she demands. "None of that. Now, you greet her and sit down and talk to her like you know you should. I'm...going to get a drink with —"

"Must you?" I refrain from throwing my hands up in the air.

"Yes I must." She glares in return, heading towards the door.

"God, it's not bad enough you're leaving me here with her, but you're going to go get drunk with that man who slaps you around like a prostitute in the Red Light District. It's not enough I have to suffer through this when I get home, but then I'm going to have to take care of your wounds after you go 'get a drink'. Fucking seriously? I can't do this today. Let me rephrase that. I'm not doing this today."

"Yes you are."
"No."
"Yes."
"No."
"Yes Connor! You have to."
"Why?"
"Because I'm your mother and I said so."

I shoot her a sarcastic look. "That might work if I were five and not the actual adult in this situation."

With a growl she buttons her black jacket up. "Fine. Do it as a favor to me."

"You let this into our home. Why the hell would I do you any favors?"

"Because it's what a good son would do." Her guilt card is one I can never manage to resist. "And at the end of every day, no matter what I've said or done, how hurt or upset you are, you are a good son..."

"Fine." I give my face a quick scrub with my hand. "Fine."

"Thank you," she mouths before sliding out of the front door.

The moment my mother's gone, I receive a look of innocence from the face on the couch. A look that I once bought, but never will again.

"You can go now too." I point to the door behind me.

"You don't even wanna talk to me?" her plea is one that once upon a time I couldn't have handled. It would've had me tripping all over myself, desperate to be the one to make her happier. To have her on top of me letting my dick make all the sadness disappear.

"About what Ashley? How you strolled into my life, fucked me, and then left me with a daughter to raise all alone at 15?" I snap, leaning against the wall beside the door. "Which by the way, she's doing amazing thanks for asking."

"Is she?" the hopeful look makes my stomach churn.

"Don't," I quickly snap. My eyes land on the ground unsure how much stability I have left in me. "Don't pretend you fucking care."

"I do care."

"No you don't," I growl again. "Don't even...just don't."

"Connor--"

"You've never fucking called. Or sent a text. Or a fucking email!" My wrath explodes. "If you had, if you had taken just one fucking moment to think about her instead of yourself, you might know some basic shit about her. Like she's on the learning levels of a four year old, just having turned three. By the way she had a great fucking birthday."

"Did she?"

"You'd know what kind of cake she had for it if you were here! You'd know she just started dance classes on Tuesday at her preschool. You'd know the name of her fucking school! You'd be able to look me in the face and tell me her favorite movie and the only thing she's ever wanted to be when she grows up is a goddamn butterfly."

Bewilderment appears on the woman who's only given Mak a little of her coloring, but no other dominant features. "A butterfly?"

"Yeah."

"Why?"

"Butterflies are her favorite creature because they're beautiful and free. Free from everything with nothing to fear as well as nothing holding them down. She wants to be a butterfly to fly to see God and ask him why her mommy didn't love her enough to stick around." My head rests against the side of the wall.

Ashley looks as if she could cry, "I…"

"Oh don't even," my eyes roll at her. "Just don't. You didn't have to run away! You didn't have to leave her! You didn't have to abandon her and never look back! All of that was your fucking choice, so I never wanna see you shed a damn tear about her."

"I—"

"You shouldn't even be here right now. You really should go."

"I—"

"You have no right Ashley. No right to be here."

"I gave birth to Kayla!"

"MaKayla!" I scream in return. "MaKayla. And congratulations for doing at least one thing right in your life."

"I am her mother Connor!"

Offended I pop up off the wall. "You are not her mother! I'm her mother! I'm her father! And I'm Goddamn Santa Claus as well as the fucking tooth fairy until some spoiled eight year old brats tell her otherwise. You…" My head shakes in fury. "You're nothing more than the womb that carried her for nine months."

Her bottom lip trembles, "What do you want me to say? Sorry?"

"If I cared, it would be a good place to start."

"You know I'm sorry Connor. I didn't know what I was doing back then…"

"Oh and I did?" I defend myself. "I had an instruction manual on how to be a teen parent!"

"I was scared!"

"And I wasn't? God, you still act like you were the only one in that situation Ashley! You weren't okay? I was in it too! I had no idea what to do! I wanted nothing more than to run away like you did, but I didn't. I stayed. I grew the hell up because I know what it's like not to have a father and thanks to you now my princess knows what it's like not to have a mother!"

"I'm sorry Connor!" She screams back, her dark brown shoulder length hair whipping side to side.

I try to regain some composure realizing all the yelling is going to wake Mak up even though she's usually a pretty hard sleeper. With a deep breath I sigh, "Will you please just leave?"

"No." She insistently shakes her head as tears fall. "Not yet. I wanna talk."

"We have. Just now." My shoulders shrug. "We're done."

"I wanna talk about MaKayla."

"She's fine. Pretty well adjusted given the fact her mother deserted her. She's better off not knowing you exist."

"She needs a mother."

My voice can't help but mumble, "She has a mother."

"Excuse me?"

"Nothing." I clear my throat and head towards the kitchen, the distance a must. How much more shit am I gonna leak out without meaning too?

"No! I heard you," she calls to me. "What do you mean she has a mother? What'd you do? Replace me?"

I lift my head from staring at the kitchen counter and stare at her through the bar window. "Let's just say someone loves her and is taking care of her as much as I am now."

"So you did replace me?"

"Replacing you implies you were there to be replaced."

"Does MaKayla call her mom?"

Refusing to answer I press my lips together.

"She does, doesn't she?" I stay silent. Leaping off the couch, Ashley rushes to yell at me through the bar window. "Answer me!"

"Yes!" I break. "Yes! She calls her mommy! She acts like her mother so it fucking fits!"

"That's bullshit!"

"That's fucking reality."

"I wanna be there for her!"

"You're a couple years too late."

"No I'm not."

"Yeah Ashley you really are." I shake my head. "You coming back into our lives would be a big mistake, and I'm already a little busy paying for the last mistake you caused, so do us all a favor and do what you did the first time and walk away."

Her light brown eyes stare at me as she whimpers, "Is that how you remember our relationship?"

"What relationship?" my fingers clink the counter. "We got together to have sex. I wanted to be committed to you, to save you from everything I thought was hurting you and you wanted to sleep with half the school, which you did. And—"

"No you wait! That's not fair—"

"That's not fair? No what's not fair is you sleeping with everything that threw a couple dollars at you like some sort of hooker. It's not fair I had to not only have a daughter right before I turned sixteen, I had to make sure I didn't have a disease too. It's not fair that I've dedicated my entire life to raising a child on my own. It's not fair you walked out and left a newborn baby without so much as a goodbye. *That's* what's not fair."

Watching her eyes water up again, I scan her face that's aged so much from the last time I saw her. She's got age lines that my mother has, which is badly being covered by cheap make up, and her complexion looks washed out, something I've learned happens from too much drug usage. My mother's a drug addict. My daughter's mother is a drug addict. My daughter's temporary mother is a recovering drug addict. What the hell is wrong with me? I asked Gianna once why she lives to hurt herself. I should've been looking in the mirror.

"Being with you was one giant mistake resulting in one amazing miracle. One amazing miracle I will not let you take away from me."

"I don't want to take her away." She sniffles wiping away the wetness on her cheeks. "I just want to be a part of her life."

"Why? Why now? What could've possibly happened to you to make you want to be a part of her life?"

She slightly shrugs, "I was sitting in church when—"

"Church?" my voice slightly chuckles. "You've found God and *now* you feel you want to be in her world? Now you want to 'right the wrongs' you've done? Look for forgiveness? Shocking."

"No," Ashley snaps. "It was more like I was sitting in church and the scripture touched me. Then a conversation I had with a close friend who ended up in the same position I was once in. She just made me realize that I needed to be a part of my child's life before it was too late to look back."

"It is too late."

She nods slowly. "I knew you'd say something like that. That's why if we can't settle this here, I'm willing to go to court to file for custody."

Shocked at her tactic, I raise my eyebrows and fold my arms. "I'm sorry. See, I've already done that. When you disappeared for an entire year I gave up hope and went and got the rights to *my* daughter. You missed the trials and custody was awarded in my favor…so."

More stunned than before I simply watch as she whines, "You can't do that!"

"I can. And I did."

"Come on Connor have a heart!"

After staring at her for a few moments I decide the only way to end this shit storm that I can barely even qualify as a day is to curl into my bed, shut my eyes, and pray for guidance out of hell hole I've fallen into.

"Look Ashley, I've already had a really long night, and you being here has been like shooting off fireworks during the worst drought in the history of existence, so if you could please excuse me I'd like to go to bed and check on my daughter." I make my way towards the front door to let her out when she grabs my arm.

"Connor please! Please, just think about it okay? Or let's talk again in the morning or something. I wrote my number down on the coloring book. Please. I wanna see her even if only for one day," she begs. "I need to see her..."

Feeling my heart ache, compassion dying to sprout, I open the front door, before it blossoms further. "If I change my mind, I'll let you know. Goodbye Ashley."

"Good night Connor." She gently touches my chest before slinking past me out of the apartment.

I shut the door with a quiet click and walk back towards my bedroom hitting every light switch on the way hoping the dark will bring ultimate blissfulness of some sort. Crawling into bed next to Mak, I pull her in close to me, nuzzling my face beside hers. I do my best to try to sleep but lay awake as time seems to drag on. The only thing to bring me comfort when my heart aches entirely too much to bear, is stroking MaKayla's soft peaceful face. Everything I do, I do for her. And I need to start remembering that.

Chapter 14

When the sun finally starts to leak through the blinds I let my eyes start to close making the grown up decision that today, I'm not going to go to school and neither is MaKayla. At least not until my shift.

Around the time I should wake up for class, my mother pops her head in the room, "Connor you need to—"

"No."

Taken off guard, not even aware that I'm awake she starts again, "Connor you need to—"

"No."

"Connor you need to—"

"Shut up," I grumble pulling the blanket over my body.

"Connor—"

"Not today Mom. I'm not going to school and neither is Mak until I have to go to work."

"But—"

"You may be able to fight your hangover and venture into work, but I had a very traumatic night and would prefer to be left alone for the day. All day, but since that's not a possibility because we have bills to pay, I would at least like the courtesy of being left alone until my shift starts. Now, good night." I snuggle down deeper in the sheet.

After a long pause, her voice whispers, "Wanna talk about it?"

"Not even a little bit."

Not knowing how to respond she simply sighs, "I don't have a hangover because I didn't drink."

"I'm thankful for the attempt to make me laugh mom but—"

"I'm serious Connor," she slides into my room a little further. "I didn't drink."

"For some reason I don't believe you," I reply from underneath my pillow.

"You don't have to. I didn't get a drink last night, and I broke it off completely with your stepfather."

Ripping the pillow off my face I sit up and sigh, "You did what?"

"I broke it off last night." She licks her lips slowly. "And I decided that I'm going to start going to AA meetings and maybe rehab, well a rehab like program or something. We make hardly enough for the lifestyle we need, me going to an official program isn't likely, but there are alternatives that are less costly."

"There are." I confirm. Confused I raise my eyebrows, "But why? Why now? Why'd you decide to quit? Why now all of a sudden?"

She points to my peacefully sleeping daughter. "I don't know, Connor. There's something about realizing I've ruined one child's life that really makes me not want to ruin another."

"Yeah?" My voice croaks. "And what brought on this realization?"

"That girlfriend of yours sure has a way with words sometimes."

Propping myself on my elbows I whisper, "What's that supposed to mean?"

"The other day we were doing dishes together while you and Mak were playing in the living room and she said something that just..." my mom's voice trails off. "We'll talk about it later okay? For right now, I have to get to work. You enjoy your day, rest, and we'll talk more when I get home. Okay Connor?"

"Sure." I nod in slight confusion.

The second she shuts the door I flop my head back on the pillow. Gianna did the one thing I haven't be able to since my father died. She got through. To my mom. To me. To Mak. And now I have to fucking let her go? Just walk away before all the good she's done turns to shit. How the fuck does that seem fair? How am I supposed to have faith through something like this?

A few minutes later. MaKayla rolls over and wakes me up to have breakfast. I fix French toast, bacon, and eggs, before I set her up to watch movies with her new doll, color, and turn the living room into her play area while I nap in and out on the couch until early afternoon when I've had enough rest. At that point I grab my phone out of my backpack.

Noticing the numerous missed calls and texts from Gianna, I do my best to merely clear the list and call Nelly feeding her a small lie about Mak running a fever. I'm dismissed for the day, but I promise to make it all up on the weekend, extra hours if needed. As soon as she lets me call out, I hang up, and toss my phone aside only to hear a knock at my door. MaKayla's attention turns from the movie she was watching, to me. Confused, who could be knocking on our door in the middle of the day. I hop up to answer it.

"Is it Mommy, Daddy?" Mak asks, her fingers died from coloring with markers. "I hope it's Mommy. You were so mean to her last night."

"I was not," I argue.

"Uh-huh."

"No-huh."

"Uh-huh." She gives me a scolding look.

Not getting anywhere by arguing with a three year old, I check the peephole to exactly what I knew was knocking.

Cracking the door, I harshly snap, "What?"

Ashley stares at me with her face frowned, her dark brown hair falling against her now thin unattractive face. She's so different than Gianna. How did I ever see this as attractive? "No hi? Seriously?"

"That is not a welcoming greeting. You are not welcomed. I repeat. What?"

"I just..I thought I'd see if you were home and…"

"And stop by?" my voice croaks. Glancing behind me I crack the door back closed not allowing Mak to see the stranger. "Why would you think I'd be at home in the middle of a school day?"

"I um…well…"

"What would you have done if I wasn't?"

"Well…see…I…"

"What do you want, Ashley?"

"I just wanted…"

"To see her." I lick my lips. "I know exactly what you want Ashley. I'm not dumb. At least not anymore."

After a slow nod she sighs, "You know Connor, I deserve that much. I deserve to see her."

"You don't deserve anything," my cold tone settles in my own veins. "You don't deserve to see her. You don't deserve to be in her presence. Get off my door step."

Her voice whimpers, "Connor…"

"Go."

"Connor," she whispers again.

Ignoring her I put a fake smile on my face, "Okay…thanks for stopping by."

"Look—"

"Daddy," Mak's voice chirps at the same time she tugs my pants.. "Daddy…Daddy…is it Mommy, Daddy?"

"No."

Ashley looks stunned by my answer.

Mak tries to open the door, "Who is it?

"Hold on," my insistence just causes her to pull on my pants harder.

"But Daddy," she whines, which is when I swoop her up into my arms to prevent her from pantsing me. "I just wanna know who's at the door…"

For the first time since she abandoned us, Ashley's eyes fall on our daughter, tears quietly pouring. The sight makes me burn hot with a rage Mak doesn't need to see. That I don't need to feel. That I am tired of fucking feeling.

"Why's she crying?" Mak lays her head on my shoulder, her hair tickling my neck.

"She lost something years ago and it's given her a case of the boo-hoos."

Accepting the answer as if gospel, she replies, "Oh…it happens. Not good to lose things."

"You wanted to see her," my voice sighs. "Now you have."

With a shaky hand she reaches out to touch her, which is when I move back, startling them both. "She's beautiful."

"Thank you," MaKayla giggles. Like the inquisitive yet blunt thing she is, she asks, "Who are you?"

"I'm…I'm…" Ashley looks at me wondering if she should say it or wait. She should never say it. She should never even think it. "I'm…."

"She's coming in," another sighs escapes me as I move to allow her to come in the apartment.

"I am?" her heart looks like it skipped a beat.

I nod allowing her to enter. Knowing I'd rather end this nightmare now than drag it for weeks, I whisper, "Yeah."

The three of us settle down on the couch, MaKayla still in my lap as Ashley stares at her in awe, waiting for me to make the moves she's been dreaming about for only God knows how long. Ones I used to want in the beginning.

"MaKayla," I push her hair behind her ear as she smiles at me happily.

"Yes Daddy?"

"You know how you used to ask me about your mommy and why she went away?" She nods, still smiling. "Remember, you used to ask if she'd ever come back?"

"Yes," I open my mouth to continue but she cuts me off, "but I know now why that mommy went away."

My face scrunches, "You do?"

"Yes!"

"Why?"

"So that Gi-Gi could be my mommy," she giggles. "The best Mommy. So we can get to Happily Ever After."

In an airy voice Ashley cries out, "Who's Gi-Gi?"

"My mommy!" Mak answers. "Daddy loves her. He was mean to her yesterday."

Quickly I snap, "No I wasn't."

"Uh-huh."

"Daddy what?" Ashley butts in.

"Loves her! She's his princess, and she even has a real castle!" she squeals joyfully. "Just like a princess should. She's pretty. I'm gonna be pretty like her. I look just like her but my eyes are green like Daddy's."

Beaming down at her for a moment, I shake my head at her innocence, but am thankful for her saying what I wish I could. "Gi-Gi is Gianna. She's my…well she's my girlfriend, or well, was my girlfriend."

"Was?" Ashley raises a suspicious eyebrow.

"It's complicated." The response causes a familiar look in her eyes. Immediately I say, "Don't even think about it. Even if we were still together or never were together. You and I are not a possibility."

"Daddy loves my mommy," Mak speaks holding a hand up. "He just got sad yesterday. It'll be okay."

I ignore her explanation and try to explain, "Mak sweetie, this is your mommy."

In the years I've been watching my princess, I've never see her face painted with so much terror and disappointed as this moment. Shaking her head she denies, "No. Gi-Gi is my mommy."

"No sweetie I am." Ashley reaches out for her.

"Fibber." Mak points a finger at her. "You are a fibber!"

"I am not fibbing," Ashley tries to defend herself.

"Fibber!" she screams and squirms in my lap. "I don't like fibbers!"

"MaKayla," my stern voice gets her attention.

With sniffles she yells, "She's fibbing Daddy. She's fibbing! We don't like fibbing! You're not supposed to fib Daddy!'"

"You're right." My lips press against her forehead. "You're right. Daddy's mistake. Calm down." She turns in my lap and clutches her small arms around my neck, tears running down to my shoulders. When she's calmed down I look at Ashley, "Satisfied?"

"Connor I—"

"You can go now."

"But--"

In a whisper I argue, "What did you think would happen? You think she was just going to welcome you with open arms? You're a stranger to her. You're nothing more than a new face. She's barely three Ashley, so she's not going to understand whatever bullshit you tell her. If you loved her like you claim you do, you wouldn't be trying to harm her and believe me, this right here, this pressure to meet her, this pressure to want her to like you, is injuring her in more ways than one. Look Ashley, just go."

Without another word she exits and I spend the next hour comforting MaKayla into a nap in our bed. I leave her there and try to pass the time playing video games on mute, the mind numbing pleasure welcomed with open arms.

By the time my mother finally gets home I'm in the kitchen preparing dinner and Mak is sitting in her booster chair brushing her doll's hair.

Lugging around the grocery bags she slams them on the counter. "A little help would be nice."

I stir the pot of pasta. "I'm sure it would be."

She shakes her head. "You're awfully cranky for someone who didn't go to school or work from the looks of it."

"Yeah well let's just say it's still been quite a rough day, no thanks to you." I snap.

"And what's that supposed to mean?" She questions, shedding her black jacket.

"That means, I owe you so very much for allowing Ashley in the house."

Her bottom lip slips into her mouth before she tries to justify, "I was just trying to—"

"I know what you were trying to do," I snap loudly. "And you had no right! It's not your broken home to fix. You had a chance to nurse and glue back the pieces to a family once and didn't, so don't go taking your regrets out on me and my daughter."

"Connor I—"

"Should've never invited her in the house!"

"But—"

"No buts Mom! She abandoned her daughter!"

"She—"

"She left her alone in this world! She hasn't contacted or even tried to be a part of her life for nearly three years!"

"I know…but she—"

"Nothing! She wasn't around for anything! She left me alone with Mak! She left me to raise her alone! To struggle to grow up! I haven't been to a prom or a party! I gave up my whole life and now that she's lived a portion of hers she wants to stroll back into ours! No!"

"Connor—"

"No!" I slam the spoon down. Fighting back tears I scream again, "No!"

My mother for the first time since my father's funeral, the last real breakdown I had like this, strolls over and wraps her arms around me for a long overdue hug. Her hold on me tightens squeezing the lingering tears out of me. I sink into her hold, arms clutching her desperately.

"It's not fair," I sob. "I've lost everything. My dad. My life. I can't do this anymore Mom. I don't wanna grow up. I don't wanna do this. I can't….I'm not strong enough. Please…please make it all stop."

On her quiet cry she replies, "Oh Connor I'm sorry." A hand strokes my back. "I know I took your father's death terribly, but I didn't know it was going to do this to you. It's my fault you're here.

Like this. And I'm sorry...I'm so sorry." The two of us quietly shed tears together until she finally pulls back and says, "I know I screwed up, but I'm gonna try to do better for all three of us okay?" I nod wiping my cheeks. "But Connor, I need you to work on forgiving Ashley."

"Why?" New tears appear, these of resentment. "Why? She's never given MaKayla anything! Not a birthday card! Not a Christmas present! Not a fucking phone call! Tell me why! Why should I give her a chance! What has she ever given to either of us?"

In the softest whisper I can recall, she sighs, "Each other..." I swallow the bitter truth. "She gave you...each other."

The sentence sounds like something my father would say if he were here trying to comfort me. And he would be right. Every terrible thing that she did brought me unconditional love from the innocence of someone I would die for. I can't imagine life without Mak and have never wanted too. Even in the beginning when all of this shit started to fall on me, from the moment I looked into eyes I know I shared, that my passed away father shared, I know I would never want to give her up.

"Daddy," MaKayla's voice yells from her seat. "Did you tell grandma about the mean lady? She was mean Grandma. So mean. And a fibber! Fibbers are bad Grandma."

My eyes fall into my mother's and she nods acknowledging neither of us are ready to deal with that subject.

"I did Mak. And she won't be back for a while. Okay?"

"Thank goodness Daddy," she overly dramatically says. "Look Grandma! Look at my new doll Mommy gave me."

Hearing her call Gianna that forces me back to the pot that needs to be drained. My mother leaves my side to talk to Mak whose mouth starts running away from her. With the conversation about Ashley dead as my tantrum, I finish fixing the three of us our first Gianna free meal in weeks. It feels awful. It feels wrong. And I know that it's not going to feel better any time soon.

Chapter 15

The next day at school I find myself hiding out in the library again. However I pick a different corner closer to the maintenance door, just in case she comes looking for me. Dodging Gianna isn't easy, but I've had my fair share of learning to avoid people. I know we need to talk, but honestly, I'm all talked out.

Leaning on one hand, I close my eyes while staring down at the book we're supposed to write our latest paper on. The peace and quiet of a noise free zone causes my brain to flutter into a silent haven. I drift off for a few moments enjoying the only restful moment my mind has taken in 48 hours.

Suddenly the book that was acting as my rabbit hole of falling into, is ripped from my grip and is lying on the floor like a dead body shot at point blank. My attention slowly gazes up to look at Gianna whose expression is similar to the one she had when we first met. This is going to be the worst thing that I've ever done.

"Paper cuts. That's all I'm saying." She stares at me blankly, so I try another sarcastic remark, "Didn't anyone ever tell you it's not polite to take things that don't belong to you?"

"Oh you mean like my heart?" She snaps clearly steering us the direction I know there's no avoiding.

"I didn't *take* your heart," I sigh reaching for the book, which she quickly steps her heel on.

"No," she hums. "You stole it."

"I didn't steal it Gianna."

"You came like a thief in the night."

"Have you been reading Shakespeare?"

"Watching," she softens for a brief second. "And if you don't call it stealing, then what do you call it?"

"A gift. Much like my heart to you, it was a gift Gianna." In a mumble I doubt she hears I add, "A gift that is going to kill me to give back."

"So that's how you treat a gift? You're careless and just…so…" her words get caught and jumbled in her throat, which is when she takes a moment to look at me to notice something. "What's the matter Connor?"

"Hm?" I raise my eyebrows.

146

"You look…you look like something has been bothering you. You look like…well honestly, kind of like shit," she sighs.

"Thanks. Not all of us can look like a model 24/7," my comment takes us both by surprise. I am clearly on a roll with this new inability to bite my tongue.

"Please don't treat me like that. I didn't mean it to be hateful I'm just saying…you don't look like yourself. You look like something bad happened. Really. Did it? Did your step father--"

"No."

"Is Mak okay?"

"She's fine." I lie. She's not fine. She hasn't been fine or stopped asking me why she can't see her Mommy and making me promise not to bring the mean lady back.

"Then what is it? What's wrong?"

"You mean aside from being harassed by your parents the other night? My daughter's mother walked right back into my life like she hadn't been gone demanding to be a part of her daughter's life once more."

"Oh my god!" Her eyebrows dart up. "You…wait what? Rewind. What happened with my parents?"

"Oh they didn't tell you?" I finally grab my abused book.

"No, they just said you… you were having second thoughts about us…which is why I tried to call you all day yesterday. And by the way, do you have any idea how rude it is not to answer or call back? Even a text message would have been okay."

"That's what they told you? That I was having second thoughts?" Shaking my head I roll my eyes. "Unbelievable…"

"What really happened?"

"After your parents basically told me I was good for nothing white trash before they tried to buy me off."

"Buy you off?"

"Yeah buy me off. They asked me what my price was to stop dating you."

"And how much did you take?"

An odd mixture of disbelief and outrage flood through me. "What?"

"Obviously you took some amount and that's why you've been avoiding me to keep up your end of the deal, right?"

147

"Can you fucking hear yourself?" I growl. "I've been avoiding you because I needed time to myself. Time to think. Just a Goddamn minute to try to understand what's going on in my world that's been turned upside down. Not because you're money crazed folks offered me a handsome reward to leave their prized piece alone."

"Snappy remark not needed. So you didn't take the money?"

"No I didn't take the fucking money. God Gianna, you think that's the reason I want you? The reason I want you around? To buy me stuff? To take care of my daughter?"

"I—"

"I told you from day from one, I don't want your fucking money. I don't need your fucking money. I'm not a charity case for the last damn time. In fact I don't need anything from you."

"Connor—"

"Just so we're clear, just so you know, just so the whole fucking world knows, I loved you because of who you are. Because I connected with something in you that I had been missing in me. Because being with you was the only thing that felt right in life outside of MaKayla."

"Loved? You said loved Connor. Past tense."

I bite my bottom lip before growling, "I did."

"So you're throwing this away? Just like that? For what? Ashley?"

"No."

"Because of my parents?"

I press my lips together. How could I be so stupid? There's no way a guy like me could end up with a girl like her. Regardless if we're the same on the inside. Fuck the fact we both know what it's like to be so alone in the world, judged for the choices we've made. None of that matters when the world gets the final say. Money does more than talks. It screams. And if Ashley falling back into our world on the same day her parents remind me of this fact, isn't a sign to give it all up, to change paths, to focus on a life I can control, that's simple, I don't know what is.

I gather my backpack and toss it over my shoulder.

In a voice that's clearly holding back sobs, she asks, "So that's it? It's over."

"Yeah."

"Just like that?"

"Just like that." I sigh and stroll away.

In a tear filled whisper I hear, "Connor wait..."

Not turning around, I continue to walk out of the library despite the pleas that are burning my soul, which just hopes I'm doing the right thing. For all of us.

To no surprise Gianna isn't in theater. Thankfully Ms. Flores doesn't make too much of a fuss and allows me to help work on some scenery painting for the freshman performance. After school and work, MaKayla and I head back to the house where I figure everything will finally be at some sort of resting peace, but am rudely mistaken. The moment I start up the steps I hear violent yelling and a different kind of screaming than I'm used too. When the hell will my life go back to normal?

Putting Mak down outside the door I look her deep into her eyes and command. "You know the drill. Go straight to the room, and wait for Daddy to get there okay?"

"Okay." She nods clutching onto her doll that is now inseparable from her.

I open the door and she flees down the hall quickly. As soon as I see the door shut I head towards my mother's room where the door is cracked and I can see the side of Paul's face. Cautiously I wait right outside, prepared to do what is typically necessary.

My mother screams, "I want a divorce and I mean it!"

"And what? Take me for half of what I'm worth?"

"No thank you. Half of nothing is even less than nothing, so I'll just stick with my half and let you go your separate way."

"Why? Why do you want a divorce?"

"Somewhere between the beatings and booze I realized that this isn't the kind of bullshit I need any more Paul. I've got a son who I fucked up pretty well no thanks to you and I'll be damned if I let my granddaughter, the only one who isn't screwed up yet, end up like him. I'd never be able to forgive myself. I'm already certain I'll never be able to forgive myself. You were one giant mistake. One giant regret. I should have dealt with Kai's death better than this."

The mention of my father's name has my head resting on the wall. It's the first time she's said it since he died. Life really is changing. Hopefully for the better.

"Look—"

"No. I don't want to hear it. I'm going clean up and get sober. I'm going to start to move past this. All this. I'm going to move on the healthy way. Take my life back. *Give* my son his life back. It's over Paul. The papers are being drawn. You are not welcomed back here."

Before he has the chance to reply, my foot pushes the bedroom door wide open. Leaning slightly in I state, "You heard her. Get the fuck out."

Admitting defeat faster than he ever has before he grouses, "What about my shit?"

"It's in a trash bag by the front door. Feel free to grab it as my son walks you out," my mother stands firm.

"My pleasure." I push up off the wall.

Paul takes one last look at my mother, glares, and heads out of the room muttering, "You're fucking lost. Good luck paying the fucking rent now."

"We'll make due," my reply receives a grunt.

I stand a couple feet back as he grabs his garbage bag of crap and storms out of the apartment. The second he's gone, I lock all three locks including the deadbolt and retreat to my mother's room. To no surprise, she's flopped down on her bed, bawling into her hands. Letting into my own emotions and understandings of her loss about my father, and having to let go of someone you care about, someone you love, I plop down beside her immediately wrapping an arm around her. She turns to me burying her face in my neck, the situation from the other night reversed. This isn't how life is supposed to be. Then again, this isn't one of Mak's princess movies. There is no happy ending.

Chapter 16

A couple weeks later, after many tense and flat out missed rehearsals from Gianna, it's time for our final evaluation before the competition. As the two of us wait to go on stage, we don't speak. My eyes can't help from stealing as many glances as possible, the old Gianna clearly settling back in. She's wearing too much make up again. Her skirts have risen to 'for sale' levels. She's even began taking the timed trips to the bathroom again, but I'm just hoping I'm being over paranoid. Once our names are called we go into the room to perform our scene, which I have a feeling is going to be the worst thing Ms. Flores sees all evening.

Not even in costume, Gianna stands on stage smacking on her gum silently.

Obviously not thrilled with what she sees Ms. Flores fiddles nervously with her hair before she asks, "Um…is there a reason you're not in costume for our full dress rehearsal Gianna?

"Nope."

"You know that's what *full* dress rehearsal means right?"

With a slight shrug Gianna adjusts her peeking bra strap, "Yup."

She shoots me a glance. Having nothing to communicate I look down. "Okay…well whenever you two are ready."

I glance at her, waiting for her to say her first line, which she doesn't until Ms. Flores clears her throat. At that point Gianna recites her first line emotionless the least amount of effort possible. After a couple more lines from Gianna like this Ms. Flores stops us.

"Um…Gianna, is something troubling you?"

"You mean like someone breaking my heart into a million pieces after you thought you could trust them?"

The bite aimed at me strings probably as deep as she hoped. If only she knew she wasn't the only one suffering from a broken heart. I wonder would it matter, would it ease any of her pain to know I can't sleep at night. That I can't stand to see Mak so sad without her around. That I can't stand being so fucking miserable without her. But I made this choice. This was the right thing to do for her. My life has to be ruled and revolves around my child. Hers doesn't. She still has that freedom. The choice.

Nodding slowly with raised eyebrows Ms. Flores asks carefully, "Do we need to start from the beginning?"

"Nope," Gianna pops her gum and shoves her hand in her black shorts pocket. "You stopped us remember?"

"Right," Ms. Flores glances at me and shakes her head in sympathy. "Continue."

When our dreadful scene is finally over, she simply dismisses us until it's our turn to hear the review. While we wait, the proper thing would be to talk to each other, but instead she distracts herself with her phone clearly uninterested in making any conversation. I fight the instinct to check on her well-being by checking on my baby girl instead who is spending the evening with Nelly since my mom is at an AA meeting. What feels like an eternity later, Ms. Flores calls us into the classroom, making sure to request for us to shut the door. The two of us sit in the seats across from her, waiting as she flips to our page.

With a disappointed look she sighs, "Would you like me to be completely honest with you on your performance?"

No. I wouldn't. I would like the rule of honesty to banished from my life because it never ends with something I want to hear. Never ends with something that gives anyone hope.

Sheepishly I reply, "Yes ma'am."

"What the hell was that?" She snaps throwing her pen down. "Here I am, impressed by the progress you two had made, impressed at how bonded you two became with each other and your characters, impressed at how in class you look like you're about to leave everyone else behind, yet, here you are in front of me putting on a scene that I could give to my freshman and have them do better than what I just saw. So I'm going to ask, again, what the hell is going on?"

My attention glances at Gianna who looks guilt free, which is when I sigh, "I…we…It's been a rough couple of weeks."

"That's no excuse Connor," she quickly snaps at me. "And given your situation outside of school I know that's not something you're used to hearing. Do you know how many greats went through hard times? Slept in their cars? Were homeless? If you want that scholarship as much as you said you did, as much I believe you do, drop the thought that life is going to pave a perfect path for you when you need it to and start paving it yourself." I don't respond. I'm not sure I know how. "You two need to talk to each other. I can sense an enormous amount of tension. I have been able to for several classes now, but I had faith you would work it out on your own. Clearly, again, I was mistaken. So here I am, heavily *suggesting* you talk about what's bothering you two and don't throw away not only a golden opportunity for both of you on that stage, but a life learning experience for you off." Sitting up straight, she waves a hand. "You two are dismissed."

The two of us exit the room, heading the direction of the student parking lot. Before reaching the door she glances over her shoulder, "Well this was fun, but I have an actual life to attend, so I guess I'll see you tomorrow."

"Wait." I stop her from walking out the door by rushing in front of it. "I wanna talk. We need to talk."

"Yeah, I'm not really in the mood."

"Yeah, well I am."

She places a hand on her hip. "And I don't really care. So if you'll excuse me." Gianna waves her hand for me to move, but stubbornly I don't. Instead I fold my arms across my chest. Annoyed she sighs, "I will kick you in the nuts if I have to."

Instantly I miss when nuts references were sexual instead of violent. "Then do it. And after I'm done crying like a bitch, I want to talk."

Gianna fights the urge to smirk. "About what?"

"Us. This. Everything that's going on."

"Last time I checked there was no 'us' Connor. You made that crystal clear. That's really the only thing it can mean when someone says it's over."

"Is that what all this is about? You're pissy because I broke up with you, so you think sucking at something that's important to me is going to fix the pain you've got?"

"Spare me your pep talk and speeches please. I need to get home. There's Netflix to watch. People to judge."

"Gianna," I state firmly. "Do you not understand what you're doing? I mean *really* understand?"

"Um…trying to leave and repeatedly being stopped?"

"I meant with this whole throwing our scene away."

"Oh. That. Nope. Not a clue."

"There's repercussions."

"Don't care."

"Damn it Gianna," I groan shutting my eyes. "You're so...so damn selfish. Fuck, don't let me forget to mention spoiled."

The sound of her scoff, shoots my eyes open as she raises a finger in disbelief. "Excuse me? Did you just call me selfish?"

"Yes."

"Let me get this straight." She drops her purse on the floor and steps dangerously close to my face. The scent of her vanilla perfume overthrows my senses. I can feel it luring me to touch her. I wanna touch her. I wanna kiss her. I wanna undo all the bad shit that's happened. But I can't. "You break up with me for whatever stupid reasons and then when I express my unhappiness with it I'm selfish?"

"That pretty much sums it up."

"Oh *please* explain that to me. It's gotta be good."

"You're being selfish because all you're thinking about is you. Your pain in this situation. How much you hurt. What about me? How I can't sleep at night without you? How Mak wakes up crying, reaching out for someone who I don't have the heart to tell her isn't coming home?" Suddenly Gianna takes a step back as if seared by the words. "Let's not talk about how hard it is for me to eat or how hard it is to have no answers for the little girl who just wants to know why her new Mommy, the only mother she's ever known can't come back to play. Let's ignore all that and remember the reason that this scholarship matters so much. How if we win, if I get this scholarship then a little girl whose lived a shit life gets a shot at a better existence. That she gets reminded that nothing can stand in the way of your dreams. That it's okay to dream big. That the world doesn't decide your fate for you," the last sentence stops me as I realize that's exactly what I've let happen to me. I let Gianna's parents decide our fate. Ashley. My mother. Everyone in the world has been making choices and influencing my decisions. Have I stopped and just thought for a second? Really thought about what I wanted and the direction to go without fear of disappointing someone? Without fear of how it could possibly end up? Here I'm thinking everything I do is for Mak, forgetting the most important thing I can ever teach her is that life is about living. About being happy. And the one time we were both truly happy, I gave it up. I gave it up because I was afraid. I'm a coward. I'm the selfish one.

"I'm asking you to show up tomorrow and give a little girl one last stride of hope she can't get anywhere else." Pushing my back against the door, I mumble a goodnight before jogging to my car, tears seconds from revealing themselves.

After picking MaKayla up from Nelly's, she spends the entire car ride hammering on about Nelly's children who took her to do so much after school. She gushes about going to the park and picking flowers. How they had chicken nuggets for dinner but they aren't as good as her mommy's. The conversation pulsates through my veins until I feel numb enough to collapse.

MaKayla's head falls on my shoulder outside the front door to the apartment. "Daddy...I really missed you."

"I missed you more." I kiss her head.

"Time for night night?" she yawns.

"Yup. Straight to bed for both of us. Daddy has a big performance for school tomorrow."

"My school."

"Mine."

"Can I come see it Daddy?" Mak asks as we walk in, the same time my mother walks out of her bedroom in her robe.

"See what?" My mother asks.

"Grandma!" She squeals in my arms. "Daddy's gonna be in a performance tomorrow!"

"That's right," she strolls over, kisses Mak's forehead, and then my cheek. "That's why Daddy had Ms. Nelly take care of you tonight. So he could practice one more time."

"Can I come see it Daddy? Please. Please! I'll be a good girl!" She bounces in my grip preventing me from walking any further.

"Of course Princess. Grandma is going to bring you and if Ashley wants to join for a small visit she can."

"I don't like the mean lady," Mak pouts.

"I know," I softly sigh. "I don't either, but what does Daddy say about trying new things."

"Sometimes that's when the best things happen!" She enthusiastically says.

"Right. So we are going to try to make friends with Ashley okay?"

"I guess..." her small voice yawns.

"Can I just say one thing about this idea?"

"What's that?"

"Do not, I repeat, do not, try to fix anything from your past by giving up your future, especially anything you weren't responsible for." She lifts her lips to my cheek again, "Goodnight Connor." Kissing Mak again she instructs, "Get some sleep Princess. Big day tomorrow."

"Night Grandma," she responds before curling into my body, doing her best to get comfortable to fall asleep.

"Come on. Let's get you to bed," I whisper heading for our room, the impending cloud of confusion and uncertainty building with every breath. I've never needed faith more on my side.

Chapter 17

Watching the clock on the wall tick my life away while waiting for Gianna to show up, I try to ignore the aching feeling I have that she's not going to show up at all. I've fucked with the chance at a better life too many times. I deserve this. I hurt her. I hurt me. My hands slide in my pocket as I lean my head against the wall in disappointment. You know, it's funny how your entire life can change in a minute. For my father's it was the first time my mother drunkenly mispronounced the hula. For me, it was the sound of heels clicking across a tile floor. To my surprise, that sound seems to echo from behind me.

Quickly I turn around to see Gianna dressed in character, a look of determination on her face.

"Gianna--"

"Wait." She holds up a finger at me. "Before you say anything, I wanna get a few things off my chest. First of all, I'm sorry for what I've said and the way I've been acting. Connor I've never once in my entire life felt the way I feel about you. In fact before you, I wasn't even sure love existed let alone that I'd feel it. Then you charged into my life and the next thing I know that's all I feel. Day in and day out. It was amazing to feel so wonderful without drugs or sex being a part of it. For the first time I was able to be me. Just plain old Gianna. Gianna who likes to laugh. Gianna who likes to cry. Gianna who apparently really loves kids and never knew. I got to figure out what it meant to really be me. But I got selfish about wanting to feel good and didn't stop to think about the other people involved like your daughter who I love so much. I—"

"But Gianna—"

"No Connor, let me finish. I never stopped to think that maybe, just maybe you had motive for doing what you did. That maybe, just maybe, you had reason for breaking up with me, and sometimes it's better to let something go than to keep it. That maybe…just maybe….sometimes it's not always about doing what you want so much as what someone else needs," she finishes right as the announcer introduces our piece. "So with that said, I'm going to go out there and do my best not for you…not for me, but for that beautiful daughter of yours whose nothing more than an innocent bystander in this situation."

Those are the last words that are said before the two of us have to take the stage. To my surprise, we put on a performance so outstanding that it receives a standing ovation and a panel of pleased faces from the judges. When we slide off the stage, she rushes off to the bathroom not giving me the time to say anything. Not even thank her for putting my daughter first.

"Connor, that was amazing!" Ms. Flores giggles appearing in front of me, blocking the path to following Gianna. "I would've never expected that from the two of you after yesterday's trial run."

"I know we—"

"Were just pulling my leg weren't you? That was a very mean and a very risky joke you two were pulling. Speaking of we, where is your partner?" She taps her nude heel on the wooden floor. "She should be with us when we receive your scores."

"I...don't know," I sigh figuring she must've snuck out while Ms. Flores had me distracted. "Don't worry. I'm sure I'll find her."

"Good. Don't take too long. There are two more scenes and then this round is over. Scores will be revealed at two, and I expect you to meet me back outside the doors at that time." She grins widely and touches my cheek. "I really am proud of both of you."

"Thank you." I nod slowly and look around for Gianna, but see my family coming my way instead.

She strolls away right as MaKayla runs into my arms. "Daddy!"

Not caring who sees from my school or others, tired of hiding the most beautiful thing in my life from the outside world, I hug her tightly, "MaKayla!"

"I saw you on stage Daddy! You were with Mommy!" She giggles her pony tails bouncing around. "She looked so pretty Daddy. Just like I 'member."

"And what do you think?" I try to drag the conversation off of Gianna. "Daddy do a good job?"

"Awesome!" She pokes the tip of my nose.

"And what'd you think?" I ask my mother whose beaming directly next to Ashley who I swear has dollar signs in her eyes. All the talk about change and that look still remains. Pathetic.

"I think that if they don't give you that scholarship they're crazy." She shakes her head.

Before I have a chance to say anything else, Bret and Brent show up offering high fives for a performance well done.

"Mom, Ashley, meet my best friends Bret and Brent," I make introductions. After they shake and exchange greetings, I turn Mak towards them. "And this little troublemaker is my daughter. Mak."

"Nice to meet you Mak," Bret says softly. "High five?"

"Yeah!" She gives him a hard one.

"Oh...ouch..." he pretends to be hurt. "I think you broke my hand. How are you so strong?"

"You have to eat your Green Fingers." She wags a finger at him.

Chuckling I shake my head as Brent says, "I don't want my hand broken so how about we fist bump?" When Mak does he pretends to push far backwards, "Whoa! You are super strong!"

"I am," Mak coos at them.

"Well it was a pleasure to meet you Mak," Bret speaks up. "We have to get going. We're picking out tuxes with Brent's dad then grabbing some wings at The Hills. Wanna meet up with us when this all wraps up?"

"No need for a tux since I'm not going to Prom next week and I would say yes to wings, but I have this little princess to watch who I promised a trip to her favorite pizza place if she behaved all of my performance."

"And I did," Mak declares. "Daddy always keeps a promise."

"I do." I smile at her. Looking back at them I shrug, "Sorry."

"It's cool," Brent offers. "Maybe next time, we all get pizza? Sound okay to you Mak?"

"Yeah!"

"Just promise not to break our hands," Bret teases before they part.

Once they're a distance away my mom sighs, "They seem like good guys."

"They are." Nodding more to myself than to anyone else I repeat. "They really are."

Not only did they show up for my performance, they took meeting my daughter to an entire other level. Put themselves on the line to do something with us that she would like out of school. Have

I been fucking up my entire life by hiding her? How many more people would be understanding? How many more people would wanna be around us? Sure, shame is a hovering factor, but doesn't Mak deserve a life outside of just us?

"Well while you wait for scores, I'm going to take the little one down the road to the playground, but we'll be back before they announce you've won. When do you think that is?"

"Around two."

"We can do that right MaKayla?" My mother holds her hands up for my daughter to switch grips.

"Right Grandma."

"We'll be back before then." She smiles sweetly at me. "Tell Daddy bye for a little while."

"Bye Daddy." She waves.

"Bye Love. Give me a kiss?" My lips pout out and she kisses them. "Have fun with Grandma."

"I will. You find Mommy okay? I miss her too..."

The heartbreaking request has my eyes dropping to my shoes. After a deep exhale I look up at Ashley who is still standing beside me. "Aren't you going too?"

"I think I'm going to stick around and talk with you for a bit." She innocently shrugs. "If that's okay?"

"Sure," I answer giving up on finding Gianna. "Let's um…go outside, around the back and talk."

The two of us stroll away just as Gianna walks by to see me with Ashley. As soon as I try to say something to her, she scampers off again avoiding eye contact. Fuck. Really. Oh I can get timing like that from the movies, but I can't get the simple resolution or civil ending?

We sit outside in awkward silence in the beginning, which is fine with me. Gianna's speech is running around, trying to burrow its way into making sure I understand what she said. Her gorgeous stage made up face keeps popping in my mind, and not because of how she was during the performance, but the hurt of seeing me standing beside Ashley. I'm sure her biggest nightmare come true. I resent Ashley for a lot of things, but if she destroyed the final shot I have with Gianna, I'm not sure I can move past that. She mainly fills the conversation with useless talks about her adventures while she was away receiving a mindless nod or reply from me when the chance presents itself. Funny, how that hasn't changed either. She never asked me how was I coping or dealing. How my life was? How anything about me was other than if I was ready to have sex with her again.

A little before 2, I find Ms. Flores and have a seat with her in the rows designated for the students who were performing. She tells me how she searched for Gianna with the help of a few other students but no one could find her. A gnawing feeling starts to grumble in my gut. As the awards start, I do my best to pay attention instead of letting my mind filter through the possible hiding places Gianna could've disappeared too. When they announce that the two of us won the competition, the larger scholarship to me, the smaller one to her, it hardly registers unlike the very real anxiety of her not being by my side during its presentation. Something is wrong. I can feel it. She may hate me, but she still would've been here for this moment. I know it. I know her.

After much praise from my fellow classmates and teacher, I manage to pry myself away from everyone to meet up with my mother, my daughter, and Ashley in the lobby. During the entire walk to them, I never stop searching for Gianna. My fingers send text message after text message just as they did earlier.

"Sweetie," my mother's voice cuts into the panic starting to settle. "I have to get to my meeting, but I'm so proud of you."

"I'm proud of you too," I hug her tightly as Mak switches from her grip to mine.

"Oh stop it. Can't I just have the motherly moment this one time?" She chuckles and kisses Mak on the cheek, "Be good for Daddy."

"Bye Grandma," she waves. "I love you."

"I love you too," my mother smiles at her and then me, "Connor Kai Owens."

In a relieved voice to not only hear those words, but my full name off her tongue in a blessing instead of a curse, I say, "I love you too mom."

As she hurries off, checking her phone in the process, Ashley speaks up, "Can I get a ride home from you? I still don't have a car and your mom was sort of my ride."

"Sure." I nod. Looking at Mak I ask, "Did Grandma put your car seat back in my car?"

"Yes," she yawns, her head falling on my shoulder.

"It's nap time for you huh?" I ask pushing her hair out of her face. Receiving a nod, I snuggle against her and carry her to my car with Ashley.

Before we reach the car she's passed out cold, thumb secured in her mouth. Carefully, I buckle her in, placing the doll she's whimpering for in her sleep, back in her grasp.

The two of us get in and head off towards Ashley's parent's house, where she moved back into.

She keeps uttering word after word like she did earlier, not even acknowledging I haven't said a word back. I can't imagine how anyone can spend that much time talking to themselves. And how can you expect to help raise a child or be in one's life if all you can talk about is yourself.

"Ashley," I interrupt her ramble.

"Yeah?"

"Can I say something?"

"Sure. Anything. Just don't yell at me again okay?"

"I appreciate your interest in our daughter's life, but honestly, I'm not ready for *that*. We're not ready for that."

"We as in--"

"All three of us," I answer. "I'm not ready to just forgive and let shit slide. Mak's adjusted to a life that doesn't include you and you...well, stop and really think Ash. You've spent all day with her, tell me one thing you learned about her. Just one." Her face starts to contort desperately digging for an answer. "Exactly. You're still all about you. It's cool you've decided that you want to know your child, but it's not the right timing. Some day when she's a little older, when you're a little more mature, when I'm...more mature, I think we can handle this situation, but for now, it would be best if you gave us some real space. Got your own life all the way back together. Let me...get ours back together too."

"But Connor...she needs a mother. Little girls need a mommy."

"She had a mother," I correct her.

"Excuse me?"

"She had a mother. She had a woman in her life who gave her food, clothing, shelter, toys, but most importantly unconditional love and affection. And not just when it was convenient for her but when Mak needed it. If there was ever a day I couldn't be there for my daughter she was, would be, and will be. Gianna loves her, and I always do what's best for my daughter and it just so happens that this time it's what's right for me too."

To my surprise she doesn't put up much of a fight. "You really love her don't you?"

"I love them both."

"No, not her," she opens the door. "Gianna."

Ashley gives me a silent nod before exiting the car. The second the door slams it feels liberating. Doors shut all the time, but with faith, the kind my father always told me to have, I know another will open, or in my hopes, reopen.

I take off down the road with only one direction in mind. The short trip over, I practice my speech time and time again. Maybe if I rehearse it enough she'll just accept it. Maybe if I sound like I know exactly what it is I want, because I do, she will see it and we can start to move past this. Get back on the right path. Our path. Together.

Pulling up to the gate, I see Benjamin, the security guard who looks as stunned to see me as I am to be here. "Can I um…help you Mr. Connor?"

"I need to see Gianna."

In a troubled sigh he replies, "She's not here."

"What do you mean she's not here?"

"I mean…she's not here."

"Well where is she?" I protest, my eyes glancing in the review mirror to see Mak still sleeping.

"I can't say."

"Ben—"

"Connor, I really can't tell you."

"Benjamin, I'm throwing myself at your mercy here. I need, we need, to find her. Mak can't keep going without her. Hell I can't keep going with her. She needs me. I just..I know she needs me. Us. This family. She needs us the same way we need her."

"Mr. Connor." He leans forward on his bent arms. "You're absolutely right. I know she needs you. You were always great at saving her from herself. You could've prevented what happened today."

Terrified of the answer, I ask, "Wh-what happened today?"

Benjamin looks disappointedly at his hands. "Attempted overdose."

Suddenly my jaw drops at the same time my heart does. My hands slide down the wheel, tears suffocating the chance of taking another breath. "Bu...but I just saw her a couple hours ago. How's that possible?"

With a slight shrug Benjamin tries not to let tears develop in his eyes, the deep affection he has for what I feel her father should. "I don't know Connor. She came home and within that hour an ambulance was rushed in the gate. She's at Park West Hospital."

Once the information has sunk into my head I allow myself to drive as calmly as possible across town to the hospital. Luckily for me, MaKayla wakes up as we enter the hospital parking lot.

"Daddy, where are we?"

Determined not to cry until I know exactly what is wrong with her and the entire situation, I answer cautiously, "The hospital Princess."

Her small voice shoots up in panic, "Am I sick?"

"No angel. Mommy is."

"Her broken heart made her sick?" The question pierces deeper than I have room for. I don't know what hurts more either. How concerned she is that Gianna is in the hospital or the fact she's right. Her broken heart, that I gave her, is the reason she's here. I am the reason. This is all my fucking fault.

Ignoring her question I reply, "We're gonna go and visit her alright? See if we can make her feel better."

"I know I can," Mak declares clutching her doll tighter. "I just know it!"

Quickly, I get her out of the car. I lift my daughter into my arms, and rush inside, following signs leading us to the emergency area, where the ambulance would've dropped her off.

Arriving at the desk, I muster up the courage to ask in an unstable voice, "I'm here to visit someone. I'm not sure, which room she's in."

Her fingers stop typing to ask, "Name?"

"Gi—" My voice stops seeing her mother headed towards the elevator. Quickly, I rush the two of us over crying her name, "Cecile. Cecile!"

Turning around, surprised to see me, she comes to a sudden halt. A very clear emotion appears in her eyes, "Connor..."

"Hi," my voice manages to whimper.

"Hi!" Mak squeaks. "We're here to see Mommy and make her feel better."

Cecile looks touched and reaches out for Mak's small hand. "That's very sweet of you."

"Mommy makes me feel better, so it's my turn."

"What a big girl choice," Cecile says to her before turning to me. "Connor, I don't think you should be here."

"With all due respect Cecile you're wrong. If I had been there for her, she wouldn't be here now. She needed me and I...I made a mistake. I'll never make that mistake again."

"Did you cheat on my daughter?"

"No." Relief flushes her cheeks. "I let things that didn't matter stand in between us instead of remembering what matters most."

"Which is what exactly?" Cecile folds her arms across her chest.

"The love we feel for each other. The happiness we can only find in each other. I can't live without her. Mak can't live without her. Please don't make us."

Breaking out into tears she tosses herself into my arms, "We were so wrong Connor. We should've never tried to rip you apart." I encourage her with a gentle pat to continue. "She was so much happier with you. So healthy. Finally becoming the person I knew she could be underneath it all...."

In a whisper I ask, "What happened Cecile?"

"Gianna came home right after your scene and went straight to her room. I thought she was just still upset about your break up, so I tried to keep giving her space. She's stopped therapy, so I told myself that this was going to happen. That she was going to shut herself away like she did every time we've moved. Like when we first moved here...but then I heard screaming. Margret, the maid, started shouting to call 911. Screaming that Gianna wasn't moving. There was an empty prescription bottle with the label peeled off a

165

few feet from her body. They've manage to pump her stomach and stabilize her."

"Can we see her?"

Cecile gives my arm a gentle rub and, "I think that'd be best. Follow me."

After a silent elevator ride and a swift walk down an empty sterile hallway, we arrive at Gianna's room, my throat swelling shut at the sight of her stone cold lifeless body.

Immediately Mak whimpers, "Daddy, what's wrong with Mommy?"

"She's just sleeping." I pull her closer to me. She has to be. That's the only thing she can be. She's going to wake. She's going to be okay. She has to be. We have too much left to live for. Too much to still share. Too much...everything.

"But I want to play with her…"

"Me too." I nod slowly, tears filling my eyes, again. Sniffling them away I try to steady myself for her sake, "But she's resting. She needs a long nap to feel better. So we're gonna be extra patient. Do you wanna wait with Daddy?"

With a sad face she nods and I sit her down in the chair while I remain standing.

"I'm gonna sing to her Daddy! Singing makes everything better." Mak explains before she softly starts singing one of the songs from her princess movies.

Taking a step away, motioning for Cecile to follow, I whisper, "How long do they expect her to be like this?"

"They say any time now, but it could be a couple more hours. It shouldn't be days but...you know how these things can go."

Rubbing the back of my neck I let out another deep sigh, "Guess we're waiting then."

"You're going to stay? I mean MaKayla has no toys. No food. What are you going to do? Eventually she's going to need both of those things?"

Shrugging I answer to the best of my ability, "I don't know. I'll figure it out. I'll spend the few bucks I have on food and she can watch videos on my phone until the battery dies."

"And bed time?"

"I'll do something about it when it comes, but it's not here yet. And our main concern right now is to be here for Gianna when she wakes up. She's gotta know we're here for her."

"Connor you--"

"What the hell are you doing here?" Gianna's father's voice breaks through.

Immediately her mother snaps at him, "Watch your tone Donald. His daughter is in the room."

"Neither of them should be here." In a low grumble he demands, eyes on mine, "Get out."

My eyes stay planted in his. "Cecile, could you please take Mak to get a snack from the cafeteria while I have a word with Donald."

"Brilliant idea," he agrees glancing at his wife.

"Mak, would you like to go get some ice cream with me before Gianna wakes up?" Cecile offers.

"Yeah!" She hops out of the chair. "Chocolate."

"Sounds good," the two of them exit the room on a fit of giggles from my daughter who is trying to weasel her way into sprinkles on the desert.

The moment we're alone he opens his mouth, "You--"

"No." I cut him off immediately. "You listen. Last time we spoke I let you do all the talking. I understand your concern. I have a daughter of my own. No man in this world will ever be good enough for her, whether rich or poor, smart or dumb, attractive or not. He will never measure up. It's just a fact. When you love your daughter that much, it's just the reality, which is why I will never be good enough for Gianna to you."

He slides a hand in his pocket not replying.

"But that doesn't mean I'm going to stop trying. That doesn't mean I won't spend every day for however long I have with her, pushing myself to be good enough. Aiming to be the man she deserves to have around just like I know she'll push herself to be the woman I want around me and my daughter. There's a good chance I'll never make the kind of money you do."

"More than a chance."

"I'm okay with that because money doesn't buy you happiness. I would rather be dirt poor for the rest of my life than let money turn me into the monster you've become. The man that let's his only child feel unloved."

"You have no right--"

"He's right dad," Gianna's groggy voice joins the conversation. "And I would rather spend the rest of my life in a tiny cramped apartment, working two jobs, living pay check to pay check with people who love me and look forward to being in my life every day, then spend it in the hell you call a home."

Sharply he snaps, "Gianna. You're clearly still delusional."

"I'm not." She shakes her head. "And make no mistake Father, if Connor and I can work this out, and I believe we can, that's it. There's nothing you can do or say to change my mind. Take away my inheritance. Kick me out. Disown me, but never, never question if we love each other because here it is Dad. Proof as he stands in my hospital room, at the foot of my bed, arguing for a chance to love me, the only other man I've ever wanted to love me."

"That's absurd," he hisses. "You know I care about you."

"Do I?" Gianna coughs. "When's the last time before this you noticed anything I did right? You've spent so much time being angry with me about the career I almost cost you, you haven't stopped to see I've really changed this time. That I've been trying to be better. To make better choices. To be *good* for once in my life. All I've ever wanted since I got out of rehab was for you to be proud of me. To love me for me..."

"Gianna I..." his defense seems to slip away from him. "But I thought if I gave you everything--"

"It's not about what your money can give her Donald. It's about what it can't." I step into the conversation. "And I may never be able to provide her a lifestyle you approve of, but you can bet every last dollar of your millions, she'll never question a day in my life how much I love her. How much I need her."

Donald's lip press firmly together in thought. After clearing his throat, he lets his eyes land on his daughter. "When you're out of here, we need to talk. About this. About us. About everything. You're my daughter and if you're going to act like it, the least I can do is act like your father."

"Or just *be* my father. No need to act like it." Gianna corrects easing her body up as the nurse enters the room.

She asks me to step in the hallway while she checks out. Impatiently I wait alone in the hallway, back resting on the wall on the other side of her room. She wants to fix this. We can fix this. Everything still has hope. Hope is enough for me.

A few minutes later the sound of Mak's voice echoes in the hallway, "I have a Grandma. So you can be my grandmom. Or my mo-mo! Be my mo-mo!"

"Princess," my voice warns. "Are you being nice?"

"Oh she's a doll," Cecile compliments as Mak struts her way over to me munching on an ice cream cone. With a soft smile she says, "I like Mo-Mo."

"Mo-Mo!" She squeals motioning her fingers for me to pick her up. Donald opens the door and Mak says, "That makes you Po-Po."

"What?" His confusion makes her snicker.

"Po-Po why do you look sad? Is Mommy still sleeping?"

"No," he answers and looks at Cecile. "She's awake. They'll be moving her in a couple hours to another room for overnight observation, but the doctors believe she will be fine. Starting Monday we're scheduling her therapy sessions again. We'll be making a few other changes, but that discussion is for another time."

Mak hums between bites, "Can we see Mommy?"

"For a small period of time. And then she'll need to get some rest. Understand?"

"Yes Po-Po." She smirks.

"Why does she keep calling me that?" His question is directed at me.

I give a shoulder shrug.

Cecile wraps her arms around his. "I'll explain while giving them a minute with her before I go in."

"Thank you." I nod before preparing to step into the room.

Donald stops me. "Connor."

"Yes, Sir?"

"Don't ever hurt my little girl again? Understood?"

"Yes sir." My answer allows me to enter her room again.

"Mommy!" Mak shouts.

"Princess!" Gianna squeaks back.

"You feel better? Your broken heart all better?"

The question raises Gianna's eyes to mine. "Did you tell her?"

"No. She thought of that all on her own," I sheepishly reply.

"Daddy's good at fixing things. Let Daddy fix your broken heart okay? I wanna play. I've missed you Mommy!"

Softly I ask, "Mak can you give Mommy and Daddy just a few seconds to talk alone?"

"Okay," she agrees. "Kisses first Mommy." Leaning her over I let Mak kiss her on the lips and sigh, "Glad you're almost better."

"Thank you."

I put her down and instruct her to ask Mo-mo to watch her for a few minutes while we speak alone. With her head held high she stomps out and makes the announcement that we need to be alone to finish fixing her mommy's boo-boos.

The door shuts and Gianna sighs, "How could she have gotten so much bigger? I just saw her a couple weeks ago."

"She grows fast. Too fast sometimes," I softly reply. "And how do you expect to keep watching her grow if you down a bottle of pills? I thought that was selfish shit before Gianna, but this..Mak's already lost one mother don't make her lose two." A choking noise comes from her throat, her eyes filling with tears. "I want you in our lives as much as you wanna be here, but that little girl always comes first, even if that means I have to walk away from you again, which isn't what I want. But we can't survive losing you to something like suicide because you couldn't find a healthy way to deal with your pain. So before we keep talking, before sink or swim, swear to me you'll never put us in this position again. Any of us. Your parents and self included. Swear."

In a choked sob she pleads, "I swear."

"Good." My hand folds with hers. "Because I love you and I don't think I could live without you. Trying to nearly killed me. And you. Gianna, I'm sorry for...for what happened, but I swear I was just doing what I thought was best for everyone. I thought letting you go would let you find the right guy with the right money and would stop Mak and I from getting hurt, but I was wrong. I was so wrong. I'm done making excuses though. I could tell you how I did what I did because of this and that but the simple truth is, I make my choices. That one wasn't right. Leaving you would never be right. So if we can, if you want to, I wanna...I wanna be like we were. Together. All three of us."

"What about Ashley?"

"What about her?" My face scrunches. "She's never been a real factor. *You* are my daughter's mother if you'll still have us. And some day, very far away, when I hate her less and Mak can understand what's going on, we will make the choice what to do about her as a family. Together." Her hand squeezes mine. "Everything is an 'us' decision from this point on. We talk about everything. Sadness. Sex. Sandcastles. All of it. We talk...together."

"Yes." Gianna nods tears falling. "Together."

"Thank God." I push my lips softly to hers, making sure not to loosen our hand hold. Dad was right. Faith will take you exactly where you wanna be if you let it. And there's no place I would rather be than here with this girl in my life.

171

Chapter 18

"Thanks again Nelly." I wipe the sweat off my forehead, throwing the bag over my shoulder. "I mean, I can't take Gianna to prom, so I'm gonna use this extra cash to take her on a romantic dinner."

"With a kid?" She skeptically looks at me from the porch, hands patting her stomach. "That's not romantic. I'll tell you what. I'll watch Mak while you two go grab something to eat, just the two of you."

"Nelly I can't ask you to do that. You've already done too much for us."

"You're not asking," she corrects. "I volunteered. Now why don't you go grab a quick shower in the guest bathroom and you can just leave straight from here."

"Thanks Nelly. I'll just chuck this and do that. Where is Mak now?"

"She and Victoria are having a tea party. You know how much my kids love her," she coos.

"You know how much I love you." I wink.

She giggles and tosses a hand at me. "Oh stop your flirting and go grab a shower."

I chuckle and relocate the trash bags to the trashcan before heading inside their two story house to the upstairs guest bath, my spare clothes in Mak's bag I carry around. I've learned from Gianna it's always wise to have a change of clothes handy for emergency situations. After a quick rinse off and scrub down in the shower, I hop out, wrapping the towel around my waist. In the months we've been together we've never just had a date the two of us, which is crazy. How many couples have never been on a date just the two of them? Not normal. Funny thing is...I wouldn't trade our abnormal relationship for one minute of anything else. There's something about everything that happens between us that just fits. And when the shoe fits who am I to complain?

Opening the bathroom door that connects to the guest room, I'm surprised when I don't see my bag on the bed any more. Damn it Mak. Always taking the entire thing instead of just what she needs from it. She calls it her purse and insists she has to have it by her all the time. If she wasn't the cutest thing in the world I think it might drive me crazy, but it makes her happy and is typically harmless so why object. Except now when I'm basically naked with nothing to throw on.

I crack the bedroom door and yell, "MaKayla Ashley bring Daddy back your purse!" Yeah. That sentence is one I'm glad my friends didn't hear me say. There would be no way to redeem myself from the embarrassment even though they are understanding.

Mak comes around the corner holding one of Nelly's hands. Confused I glance at Nelly's other hand that's gripping some sort of garment bag.

"Sorry Nelly, I'm not..." My head bobs around for the right word to say. Last thing I need is Mak repeating the word naked everywhere. "Decent."

"I know," she snickers. "I'm bringing you something to put on."

Holding out the bag for me, I quickly read the word 'tux'. "That's not mine."

"It is yours Daddy!" Mak claps her hands together. "You're going to the ball Daddy! You're going to the ball."

"What ball?" I tilt my head at her and then look at Nelly. "What ball?"

"Pom!" Mak squeaks. "Your ball is called Pom!"

"Pom? You mean Prom?" Looking at Nelly I snap, "Does she mean Prom? What does she mean I'm going to prom? I'm not going to prom. I can't afford that. I can't--""Can't. Can't. Can't," Nelly mocks me and shoves the bag at me again. "It's not about can't Connor. It's about can. You should know that. You should've learned that much by now. Now put that on and meet us downstairs when you're done. Socks and shoes are at the bottom."

I slide back in the room and toss the bag on the bed staring at it in disbelief. Gianna told me she had plans all afternoon, but I didn't think it was this. It shouldn't have been this. It's bad enough I can barely afford to take her to dinner, but the one thing as a senior I should be able to do for her, and I can't even afford it. The tickets for the two of us were a quarter of Mak's tuition. Unzipping the bag, there's a note waiting for me.

Connor,

You have been the man of this family long before you should've been. You've spent your life taking care of your father, of me, of Mak and you deserve a break, even if only for one night. Now, I know you because you're my son, so before you go off into a tantrum on how this money for a rental tux could've been better spent, remember money can be remade but memories like this can't. And you know who said that. So make your father proud and take his advice. Enjoy your prom.

We love you.

-Mom and Dad (in spirit)

Sinking onto the bed beside the tux I scrub my head with my hand. There are so many things she could've done with that money. So many better things. She just started working two jobs to help the household more. This could've been used for groceries. Gas. I glance at the note, certain words floating off the page, the sound of my father's deep voice repeating them.

In a hushed voice I nod, "Money can be remade...memories can't." With a swift look up at the heavens, where I know he's guiding me from I whisper, "Alright Dad. You win this time. Faith in you and your teachings have brought me this far, they won't fail me now."

Once I'm changed, I jog down the stairs with my tie hanging undone. Seeing Nelly and Mak at the kitchen table eating cookie dough out of the bowl, I fuss, "Mak are you supposed to eat it out of the bowl?."

"Mrs. Nelly says this is what it's for," she explains before putting her whole hand in the bowl. "Cookies are in the oven."

I shoot Nelly a look who rolls her eyes, "Oh let it go. She's fine. We're fine." She pauses and looks at the tie. "Okay, you're not. Let me wash my hands and tie that."

The sound of the kitchen sink starts at the same time Mak says, "Taste it Daddy!"

Leaning over I let her put a dot on my lips for me to lick away. "Mmm...tastes yummy. Maybe I should eat you. You taste delicious too don't you?"

"No Daddy!" She giggles. "I'm not food!"

With a smirk I turn around to Nelly who starts to tie my tie. "I want you to go and have fun. Don't worry about picking up Mak until tomorrow morning."

"Nelly--"

"Sh." She demands. "Now I got you a red corsage, so let's hope that girlfriend of yours is wearing something simple. Plan on picking Mak up at 11. We're having a girls day tomorrow morning, making pancakes and wearing our tiaras, so I don't want you to interrupt."

"No tiara for you Daddy." Mak wiggles a finger at me.

"When'd you get so bossy," I playfully fuss at her.

She smiles as she licks her fingers again.

"Be safe. Be smart. Most importantly...Have fun. Even you deserve that once in a while." Nelly pats my chest. "Now, grab the flower out of the fridge and get going. Your ride is waiting."

Touched by everything she's done for me today, every day, the understanding and compassion I needed from my mother, but hadn't been receiving has my jaw bobbing for something to say. The only thing I can decide on are two words that my dad always told me you could never say enough and when sprinkled with a genuine attitude, would be enough.

"Thank you."

With a wide smile she nods, "You're so welcome..."

I walk out and through the living room, around to the front door where I walk out to see a sight strong enough to make me say fuck prom and take her back to my apartment.

"God you're gorgeous," the words are out of me before I can think of something clever.

Gianna spins around in her short black halter top cocktail dress. My eyes drink in her long legs on display in her black heels, her curves that have expanded to a healthier level than when we first met, her pinned up hair, but most importantly the alluring smile on her perfect face.

"You like?" She saunters over.

"I love." My hands holding the corsage wrap around her waist. "You. And the outfit."

Her hands pull at the jacket, "You clean up nice yourself."

175

Immediately I open my mouth to explain to her how this isn't what I wanted. How I wanted to be the one to do something special for her. How I wanted to be the one to give her this moment.

"I know," Gianna hums out. My head tilts to the side. "I know what you're thinking, but as long as you're the one I walk into my first prom with, that's all that matters. You could take me in your old converse and jeans and I would be just as happy. It's not about money Connor. You know this by now."

"But still."

"Let it go. We're gonna have enough problems with graduating, college scheduling, apartment hunting, and making sure to not neglect Mak through all of that. Let's not add an unnecessary problem to the mix."

Knowing everything she said is the truth, I pull her into me a little tighter. "You're right."

"Did you just tell me I was right Mr. Owens?"

"Don't let it go to your head. I'm paying for dinner. Wherever you wanna go. I don't care if it's gonna cost me 40 bucks or 400. Wherever you wanna go, we're going."

"Fine!" Gianna caves and kisses me on the lips. "But just remember you said that when we get there...Come on."

Gianna and I take the limo to a hole in the wall burger joint close to downtown where Prom is being held. She insists they have the best bacon cheeseburgers and she's right. We do our best not to get our attire dirty as we share chili cheese fries and milkshakes, enjoying laughs and stealing kisses between bites. Afterwards, we put on the flower things we're supposed to be bearing and take the limo to the hotel they are holding the event in. We spend the night dancing to old 90s music intertwined with radio hits that sound so much better when Mak isn't singing them.

At various points we run into my friends. Bret whose date seems to be trying to swallow his tongue every time we cross paths, and Brent who's date looks annoyed his attention is everywhere but on her.

She storms off insisting she's going to grab some punch and I take the opportunity to help someone out in the love department. Still new territory for me, but I know enough that if I don't speak up now he'll never make a move.

"Dude, go ask Nicole to dance," I insist. "You've been staring at her all night. She's been staring at you the same. Just make it happen already."

"Shut up," Brent denies. "She hasn't."

Gianna rests her head on my chest, arms wrapped around my waist. "She has. She totally has a crush on you."

Blushing he looks down, "No. No way." His head lifts back up. "A girl like that...what would she want with a guy like me?"

"I ask myself the same question every day," the confession has Gianna looking up at me. "But in order to know the answer, you've gotta take a chance to find out. Quit being a pussy and go."

"I'm not a pussy," he grumbles scratching the back of his neck.

"It's just a dance," Gianna pushes. "Not a marriage proposal."

"You talked less as a stripper," the joke takes us back to the first time I introduced them.

When I start chuckling Gianna starts swatting at me until, I toss my arms lovingly around her. With one final nod, I insist for him to go before his date charges back at him.

"Okay. I'll go," he prepares to walk off but stops. "Before I go, my family is doing a backyard cook out next weekend if y'all wanna come."

"I appreciate the invitation, but with Mak--"

"Bring her," he shrugs. "My cousins and shit are coming and they're about her age. She's like 3 right?"

"Yeah."

"Totally. You two come and bring her, we'll hang out. I hear we're heading to the same college too, so maybe you can tell me what you think of the dorm they wanna toss me in."

"Sounds good," I agree. "Now go before you puss out."

"Yeah, yeah, yeah," he mumbles walking away.

Looking down at Gianna I sigh, "As much as this hurts my feelings to say, we should probably head home, before that limo turns into a pumpkin."

Slyly she smirks, "One more surprise Connor..."

Uncomfortable I raise my eyebrow. "Gianna...what did you do?"

"Follow me," she insists dragging me out of the room, down the hall, and towards the elevator.

"Where are we going?"

"I got us a room." Without letting me reply she continues, "I'm not saying anything has to happen, I'm just saying, it's been almost a month since I've fallen asleep in your arms and I want that."

The doors ding open and we slip inside. As soon as they shut I wrap a hand around her nape and pull her into a deep kiss. Taken by surprise she squeaks briefly before melting into me. My lips tease hers, plead with them, beg for entrance, and when it's granted I take full advantage of it.

Ending the kiss much sooner than I would've liked, Gianna happily sighs, "Our floor."

We stumble down the hallway kissing and hugging, the entire time never more than a couple inches apart. With a quick swipe of the card, the two of us are granted access to a small suite with a giant window with blinds open revealing the city to us.

The door shuts behind us and Gianna gasps, "It looks so beautiful like this."

Leaning against the door, I tilt my head to the side, "I was thinking the same thing."

She shoots me a sassy look over her shoulder. "I think you're trying to seduce me..."

I wet my lips. "Is it working?"

A tiny whimper comes out of her before she nods. Stalking over, I pull her into another deep kiss covered in unspoken I love yous and more importantly I want yous. With my fingers sliding down the back of her dress, I guide her the direction of the bed, intentions clear. We've both waited long enough for this moment, the possibility of either of us walking away from this situation non-existent. As the speed and intensity of the kisses increase, igniting my nerve ends on fire, awakening a beast that's been asleep for entirely too long, I can't help but softly smile to myself at the idea of my child being right. Her Daddy will finally get his happily ever after. It's not about the castle or the dresses, the villains or the scenery. It's about having faith in letting life lead you where you want it to go. In reality, we all get a Happily Ever After, it just depends on where you decide to stop the story.

178

Thank Yous

Crazy Lady- I love you. Thank you for everything you do for me every day by just simply being my mommy.

Her Husband- I look forward to the proud hugs you give.

The Law Student- Thanks for being there sis.

The Lumberjack- Here's to feeding my Tex Mex habit, lol

Sissy B- One of the best parts of our family.

The Doc- For all the understanding you give me, many thanks.

Real Life Erin- Dude, how are we not in Vegas yet? Lol

My PAs- Or as I call you my left and right sanity. Thank you. I know I'm a lot of crazy to deal with sometimes. I can never repay you for what you do.

The Editor- You...you love like a rib I'm not giving back, lol

The Army- You ladies remind me we can do anything together!

When I Grow Up Team- Selena Laurence, Jaime Reese, Kristine Cayne, Harper Sloan and Tess Oliver, for showing the way to me even if you don't know it.

Bloggers- I appreciate you do everything for the little guys like me. You give us a chance to grow in an industry that's always trying to stop that from happening.

Betas/Dream Team- You loves make life fun and so much better. Never forget that.

Readers- You are walking proof for anyone who thinks dreams don't come true that they are wrong. You have made mine real.

Until next time....

FOLLOW ME!!!

Facebook- https://www.facebook.com/XavierNealAuthorPage

Facebook group-

https://www.facebook.com/groups/1471618443081356/

Twitter- @XavierNeal87

Instagram- @xavierneal87

Goodreads-

https://www.goodreads.com/author/show/4990135.Xavier_Neal

Amazon- http://www.amazon.com/Xavier-Neal/e/B00IY1FR1Y

Pintrest- https://www.pinterest.com/xavierneal/

Newsletter Sign up- http://eepurl.com/bYqwLf

Company Newsletter Sign Up-

Curious about my other works?

Check them out down below!

Senses Series (Sports Romance/ Romantic Comedy)

Vital (Prequel Novella)- http://amzn.com/B01D7V5AU8

Blind- http://amzn.com/B00N96BDKS

Deaf- http://amzn.com/B00O3TTK3W

Numb- http://amzn.com/B00P58R1EK

Hush- http://amzn.com/B00QGH8OUE

Savor- http://amzn.com/B00RON0AV0

Callous- http://amzn.com/B00T3M5VNM

Agonize- http://amzn.com/B00U5PX976

Suffocate- http://amzn.com/B00VJ51PRW

Mollify- http://amzn.com/B00X1NJTAU

Box Set (Books 1-5)- http://amzn.com/B00UCIULA4

Adrenaline Series (Romance/ Romantic Suspense)

Classic- http://amzn.com/B010MX9WVC

Vintage- http://amzn.com/B011GGSQ34

Masterpiece- http://amzn.com/B014N0S11C

Unmask- http://amzn.com/B015XBBDF6

Error- http://amzn.com/B017CCHVQY

Iconic- http://amzn.com/B018IS1UPE

Adrenaline Series Box Set (Books 1-3)- http://amzn.com/B014SAQVP0

Prince of Tease Series (Romance/ Romantic Comedy)

Prince Arik- http://amzn.com/B01CUU24PG

Hollywood Exchange Series (Romance/ Romantic Comedy)

Already Written-

Blue Dream Series (Contemporary Romance)

Blue Dream- http://amzn.com/B017QQOT2K

Purple Haze- http://amzn.com/B01D7Y1HX4

Havoc Series (Military Romance/ Romantic Suspense)

Havoc- http://amzn.com/B00O8DZMIA

Chaos- http://amzn.com/B00QOI8WO8

Insanity- http://amzn.com/B00U1RWUUK

Collapse- http://amzn.com/B00WCHUUSG

Devastate- http://amzn.com/B00YF45TIA

Havoc Series Box Set (Books 1-3)- http://amzn.com/B00U1MXJ2S

Never Say Neverland Series (NA Fantasy Adventure)

Get Lost- http://amzn.com/B013C8QLJK

Lost in Lies- http://amzn.com/B00SGFLPLO

Lies, Mistrust, and Fairy Dust- http://amzn.com/B013XBV0VU

Rub Me Series (Erotic Shorts)

Rub Me The Right Way- http://amzn.com/B01110Q3C6

Rub Me The Wrong Way- http://amzn.com/B013NXMDTG

Rub Me All The Way- http://amzn.com/B0155JHKJY

Erotic Short Complete Box Set- http://amzn.com/B0157995UO

Standalone

Compassion- http://amzn.com/B01AYP3FYI (Military Romance)

Cinderfella- http://amzn.com/B00XAZ1YY8 (YA Contemporary)